Georgia Law requires Library materials to be returned
or replacement costs paid. Failure to comply with this
law is a misdemeanor. (O.C.G.A. 20-5-53)

DISCARD

All Good a Week Ago
In My Lifetime Series

Clay Church

Cadmus Publishing
www.cadmuspublishing.com

Copyright © 2022 Clay Church

Cover art by Francisco Moraga – fjmoragaproductions@gmail.com

Published by Cadmus Publishing
www.cadmuspublishing.com
Port Angeles, WA

ISBN: 978-1-63751-325-5
Library of Congress Control Number: 2023900148

All rights reserved. Copyright under Berne Copyright Convention, Universal Copyright Convention, and Pan-American Copyright Convention. No part of this book may be reproduced, stored in a retrieval system, or transmitted in any form, or by any means, electronic, mechanical, photocopying, recording or otherwise, without prior permission of the author.

This is a work of fiction; therefore, names, characters, places, and incidents are the products of the author's imagination or are used fictitiously. Any resemblance to actual events, locales, or persons, living or dead, is entirely coincidental.

Acknowledgements & Dedication

A lot of people helped me during this time and I'm grateful for that but as to this book I'll like to thank a few. First I'll like to thank two of my sisters, Nikki and Moca who both played a part in helping me get this book out I thank you and love y'all. I'll like to thank two of my brothers, Robert Harris and Jay Ross both helped me out more than anyone and this book would only be a dream if it wasn't for y'all, love and thanks to you both. Last but not least I'll like to thank Cadmus Publishing for making it easy for me to get this out...

I dedicate this book to my nephews hopefully this small accomplishment inspire y'all to give 100% to turning your dreams to reality. Knowing that failure isn't trying and not succeeding but failure is wanting to do something and not trying. I love y'all...

CLAY!

Table of Contents

CHAPTER 1 1
CHAPTER 2 7
CHAPTER 3 12
CHAPTER 4 24
CHAPTER 5 40
CHAPTER 6 50
CHAPTER 7 60
CHAPTER 8 70
CHAPTER 9 79
CHAPTER 10. 86
CHAPTER 11. 93
CHAPTER 12. 103
CHAPTER 13. 109
CHAPTER 14. 122
CHAPTER 15. 133
CHAPTER 16. 139

CHAPTER 1

"AHH FUCK!" I yell as I pop up out of my sleep. Quickly rolling to my left in one smooth motion I snatch up the pistol I sleep with and pull out the 7 inch hunting knife I keep in a sheath attached to my bra under my right armpit. Hitting the floor and coming up on one knee with both weapons drawn, I scan the room left to right... Following the infrared beam as it cut through the dark room.

Pissed knowing there's no one here. My room was empty but still having to go through the motions. "Calm down girlie, breathe." Inhale... Exhale... I repeat to myself. "GOD DAMN!" I say as I toss the pistol back on the bed. Six months this been going on, if it's not a nightmare it's lightning and thunder waking me up. Hitting the snooze button I realize two things: One, that it was time for me to get up anyway since my alarm was minutes from going off. Two, at least I didn't shoot my alarm clock like I did six months ago. Besides the jumping out of my sleep today wasn't starting off that bad. Picking up the water bottle with a smile on my face and now a bounce in my step, ready to start my Monday on a good note, I walk to the stairs and stop. Damn look at all this space, I gotta get some furniture. It's been a year since I returned from a forced absence of my life. Renting this Downtown Loft was a must-have, but it's time I start looking at this place as my home and not just a place I can duck off and sleep. It's like I'm paying $2,600.00 for a queen size bed. Not liking that logic at all. Shaking my head as I make my way to the bottom of the stairs where my greyhound Tricks waits for me.

"Alexa! Play my Zen Meditation and Natural Playlist for twenty minutes."

Standing barefoot on a yoga mat in front of my workout mirror, in a Tommy Johns all white cotton bra and panties set… At 27 no one would doubt I was once an All-American High School track star, ranked number one in the nation. Standing five feet, ten inches and 165 lbs, most of my weight shows in my thighs and legs. I notice the muscles that define my legs as I model them off and flex them. If I love the definition I also gotta love the scars that decorate my body. Starting with the buckshot wounds that run up my right light brown thigh. A wound I got in a shootout with them East Warren boys, back when I was still back on the Police Force and undercover.

Saying nothing of the scars I received from kneeing people and just falling. As always when I take stock of my body I always find myself smiling when I look at the scars that adorn my flat stomach, once a six-pack, and now a solid two-pack. Memories of when I quit the Force and was riding with the biker gang, Land Sharks. For the past two years my smile easily transforms to a menacing smirk once I lay eyes on my face. All my life I was thought of as fine. Told I looked like T-Boz from TLC, just a shade darker. Now two years removed from my face being served to Piranhas. Lucky they didn't have time to eat through my skin and tear my face muscles… Never been into my looks anyways, the scars don't bother me plus I kinda like them, makes me look more BAD ASS, I think.

Women are more attracted to my confidence and my shape. "A mouth full" cuffing my B-cups, "and more than a handful," I turn around and cuff my fat ass and watch my light brown ass cheeks bounce in the mirror as I release them. I'm still gangsta cute, I think to myself as I take in my face again. The diamond stud at the corner of my mouth and the two gold hoops hanging from my nose bringing attention to my full lips, which can find they way to a clit with no navigation. Loving the two rubies I got tattooed instead of tear drops for my dead mother, Ruby. The red looks good on my light brown skin tone and set off my brown eyes. Usually I keep my hair cut to a fade, but due to circumstances I was forced to let it grow. My native roots showing in my jet black hair which I rock one side in a single French braid. I keep the other side bald, bringing attention to my tattoo that covers half of my head. It's the Sky Line of Detroit and the words "The City is Mines" across the horizon.

"Fuck what they talking about I'm a problem."

Done with my inspection of my body I look at my watch. Fifteen minutes to clear my mind... Forgetting everything else I focus on my breathing and heart beat calming myself.

Folding myself completely I grab my ankles...

Never had 5'10" and a hundred and sixty-five pounds moved so gracefully as Vegas flowing in and out of Yoga positions.

"Ahh," stretching now it's time to get real, I think as I notice the Zen music has ended.

"Okay! LET'S GET IT!" I say hyping myself up as I jump up and down anticipating the moment my mirror comes on and DMX starts blasting from my system.

Slowly maneuvering my forest green 2020 SRT Super Stuck Charger through downtown I can't help but think about all the shit I be into as I hit a corner. Seeing the dingy grey Detroit County Jail standing there twenty-something floors high. Damn... I probably committed more crimes than any one person in that whole Jail. From robbery, selling drugs, kidnapping, to murder. I know only my knowledge of both sides and how I manipulate that knowledge is the only thing that keeps me free and barely alive at times... "You know me well/ from nightmares of a lonely cell/ my only hell/ but since when niggas known me to fail/ Fuck Naw!" Quoting my favorite Jay-Z line and giving the County Jail two middle fingers before I speed off.

Hearing my phone ring I turn Drake down to a whisper and tell Alexa to answer the phone.

"Good morning, Bae!" hearing Sara's voice brought a smile to my face.

"It's good now, sexy. Put me in position."

"That's why I'm calling, we still on?" Dropping her voice like that and knowing what she asking had me wanting to reach into my panties.

"House of Pant, room 6." Damn, saying those words bring a crazy vision of Sara's pecan complexioned body to mind.

"Ummm! Okay, Bae. I'll see you then."

"Okay Sexy, say no more."

Thinking back to when I first seen Sara standing behind the cash register at her Father's liquor store. Never had five inches looked so tall and forty-five pounds looked heavier than when I stand next to Sara's 5'5" and a hundred and twenty pound frame. I can't remember not one word that was spoken between the two of us, just that I was buying a Papaya Ever Fresh. I couldn't take my eyes from her sexy-ass lips, a shade darker than her pecan complexion, kept me thinking and betting her nipples were the same shade. Not usually finding Arab women attractive, too hairy, but that shit was sexy on Sara. The smile she was giving me that day had me thinking she was reading my mind... "Goddamn!" Shaking my head I had to turn the drake back up, thinking about Sara would have me creaming my panties as I fly down GrandRiver.

Turning down my block to my Ridgewood house, which I now find myself calling it that since I got my downtown loft. As my routine is whenever I turn down my block I scan the streets for any unrecognized cars and I check between the houses for suspicious activities.

In time you'll see that I got every reason to be paranoid, I play a dirty game out here.

ALL GOOD A WEEK AGO

Approaching my house the thing I notice first is that the gate to the part of the yard that I keep my bull mastiff "Scar" is open. Looking down the street I see my cousin's all black Ram TRX truck. Pisses me off every time I see it... That's what I get for letting that nigga know my plans.

Not slowing down I pass my house and continue my search. Not seeing nothing crazy I put my car in reverse and park in my driveway. Hopping out I'm followed by Tricks.

Dressed in a Givenchy Joggin' suit which highlights my thick lower half like most of my clothes do. Although I'm considered as a Tomboy, growing up I always embraced and flaunted my figure and like always two 9mm hang in holsters at my ribcage. Stretching and taking a minute to enjoy the spring air as Tricks finds a place to piss.

Unlike my loft my Ridgewood house feels and looks like a home somebody lives in. I take a deep breath as I kick off my Airmax 95's and head to the back room where I know I'll find my cousin grooming Scar.

"Whatup doh!" I yell giving her a heads up that it's me.

"What up, cuz." Moose says to me as I step in the doorway and see her struggling with drying an excited Scar who spotted Tricks.

"Cuz, you better get her before Scar buss her ass again!" I can't help but chuckle at that.

Standing 6'4" and dark skinned with 360 waves, Moose could easily play Chris Bosh's twin sister in a movie. As early as 8 years old the family knew that Moose was gay and was going to be what most lesbians call a 'Stud'. Since 10 she rocked a taper and was trying to turn 5th graders out.

"Nigga I see you still fuckin' wit that young bitch Porsche, know she 17 right?"

"Yeah, and she taste young and fresh too. Fuckin' the shit outta her young ass," Moose says smiling with excitement and lust in her voice. "Plus she about to be 18, but Cuz, you see her momma? Those lips! Catch her alone... get my dick and my clit sucked."

Lost in her own little world and forgetting the task at hand with her mind on Porsche and her momma, Moose forgets to keep a tight grip on Scar. He lunges toward Tricks who refused to stop prancing her narrow ass in his face, and since the room was small that lunge had him on her tail. Tricks dodges right then spins left and heads for the safety out the door around me. I let Scar get past me too before snatching him up by the collar.

"SCAR SIT!" Too excited to obey, so I smacked him on the ass, "SIT! This nigga need some pussy." When I say this we both bust out laughing, liking pussy, knowing how he feeling.

"Hell yeah! I'll bring one of them bitches from the kennel over," Moose says.

Glancing at my watch I see it's almost 9:00am. "Moose, take Tricks to Rev's for me, speaking of pussy I gotta go…"

CHAPTER 2

    Laying naked on the bed hoping to rub one out before Sara's teasing ass step in. Pussy on fire as I watch a chick on TV play with her pussy and I play with mines, copying every move she makes as I spread my thick thighs. I slowly rub my clit and pinch on my super sensitive nipples. My nipples are not very long, but my areolas are large and a super turn on for me whenever I play with my pussy in the mirror.

    "Mmmm!" Moaning as I get a close up of her glistening wet pussy on screen. "Ahh. That pussy super wet... Ohh!" Easing two fingers into my tight couchie. "Damn," I whisper as I stuff my pussy and using muscles to clutch my fingers as I pull them out. Breathing heavy, now my body is on fire...

    Sara walks into the room in a silk white robe and pumps looking sexy as hell with her hair in a top bun, lips shimmering with gloss. Leaving my fingers buried in my steaming sex rubbing up against my walls, I see Sara coming my way. I lift one of my beautiful breasts to my mouth and flick my tongue against my little hard nipple not breaking eye contact with Sara. Dying to see her body under that robe, Sara leans down and we tongue wrestle around my nipple. Oh my god it felt so crazy and exotic. Every time our tongues would touch a shock of pleasure would shoot to my pussy causing my walls to clutch my two fingers. Pulling my fingers out of my sopping wet pussy Sara sucks them into her mouth to the knuckles.

"Mmmm!" Closing her eyes and moaning around my fingers and savoring the taste. Hearing her moan had me creaming. Stepping back she let my fingers fall from her mouth and with a mind of their own they head straight for my taut nipples… Untying the robe and letting it fall to the floor I suck in a breath when I see Sara's oiled up body standing there in an all white, all lace bra with the boy shorts to match. Nowhere as thick as me, but Sara has a set of titties that's too big for her small frame. That bra looked too small, barely containing her b-cups. I look down and see a pussy so fat and wet, clearly I can see the little hair Sara keeps on her pretty pussy. Wanting only to cum in Sara's mouth still couldn't keep me from sliding my fingers back in my throbbing pussy. I was so wet now and I was wondering if Sara could hear my pussy. Whimpering and moaning with each thrust, trying to speak without words…

Slowly swaying her hips and seductively rubbing her body, pushing her lace covered b-cups together and licking between the crack.

"Damn, Sara, you so fuckin' sexy right now." I say as I spread my shaved kitty for Sara to get a good view of my throbbing clit as I slowly thumb it like a guitar string. "Uummm!" I softly moan, biting on my bottom lip. Seeing Sara lick her breast was like the ultimate tease. Knowing how soft her skin was and how crazy her tongue game was… Damn! Sara had this teasing shit down pat, my pussy was so hot and I was hating the feeling of wanting something to fill my pussy. I insert two fingers back into my pussy as Sara frees two of the firmest breasts I have ever seen… God, how they bounce on gravity like that, I ask myself. I was moaning crazy now with three fingers in my box and my palm rubbing my clit.

"Ohmygod!" Sara moans standing there pulling and releasing her hard nipples, watching me fuck my fingers as I lift my hips off the bed, humping and grinding, begging for a release. Keeping my eyes on the two puffy lips pushing against the wet stain anticipating the moment I get a clear view of that fuzzy peach.

"Owww!" I let out an aching moan seeing Sara turn around and bend over. Man this bitch got me so fucking horny. Seeing that fat pussy hanging there trapped in them boy shorts. Pulling her hands outta her panties as she looks over her shoulder at me. My pussy juices just keep gushing, she was killing me and I still couldn't cum! Licking the juices from her fingers while still looking at me. "Uummmmm! Bae, come pull my panties off."

Shit, I was at the foot of the bed in seconds slowly pulling her panties down inch by inch taking my time to enjoy the look of Sara's perfect round ass. Both of us let out a low moan once her wet pussy release the grip it had on the crotch of her boy shorts followed by a trail of sticky juices hanging from her pussy. "Goddamn!" I say as I reach between Sara's legs feeling the heat before I even dip a finger in. Closing my eyes and taking a whiff. Maybe I'm tripping but damn this bitch smell exotic. I spread Sara's cheeks and kiss them, not really into eating ass, but Sara's asshole was so pretty I had to kiss it and take a swipe.

"Ohh baby, you nasty." She sounding so sexy I had to do it again! Sliding two fingers in Sara's hot pocket I could feel Sara playing with her clit. "Vegas, Yesss! That feel sooo good. See how you got me?" Sara coos.

Pulling Sara's panties all the way off I withdraw my fingers from her pussy and clean my fingers with my tongue loving the sweet tinge flavor. Panties still in hand I get to the middle of the bed inhaling deeply on the panties before sucking on the crotch area. This bitch had me drunk. Sara turned the porno to full blast. The woman on the screen filled the room with her moans as she pulled a 10 inch black dildo out of her pussy. I spread my thighs wide and tap my pussy a few times.

"Stop playing and come eat," hearing the want and need of a release in my voice Sara gets right to it opening my light brown pussy lips. Finally having another set of hands on my body damn near did it!

"Damn yo clit so fat," Sara says.

My pussy was so wet now, dripping and forming a wet spot under my asshole. Sara starts licking my clit before covering my pussy with her mouth and humming and then pressing my juicy clit between her lips firmly, knowing how I like it.

Sara had me clutching at air. "Aahh! Uhhh!" I moan as I arch my back before humping my pelvis in her face. Sara's tongue was like a twister on my clit. "Mmmmmm, ohoh." Now I was moaning loudly enough to hear myself over the T.V. Sara firmly licks my clit and stuffs my pussy with three fingers. I lock my legs around her neck as I pull on my nipples feeling something great about to happen. I was breathing hard and moaning wildly feeling all my pussy muscles contracting around her fingers. "Ohyes, ohyes, I'm cumming… Yesss. Nowww!" Pure ecstasy rocks my body and I flood Sara's mouth…

Panting hard and still twitching as I look up at Sara. Damn that muthafucka look like a real peach. I think as she open her pussy and a drop of her juices land on my chest.

"You wanna taste?" She teased as she dipped a finger. Instantly I pucker my lips and stick my tongue out as Sara lowers herself on my face…

Slowly grinding her pussy across my face from nose to chin. "Yesss, Vegas, umph!" Sara moans as she bangs on the wall. Hearing the sound of boards shifting my pussy instantly starts creaming like crazy…

Three holes open up on the wall above my head, one in the middle and two to the side and a little higher. Seconds later a huge black dick comes out the middle hole and arms shoot out the side holes. Sara not wasting no time deep throats the dick. Seeing that I clump down on Sara's pussy and cuff her ass cheeks to hold her in place. Flicking my tongue around her clit as I massage her ass, taking turns doing that and lightly pressing her clit between my lips. Sara was moaning crazy around the dick before pulling it out and causing a loud wet sound.

"Damn! Vegas ummmm, I'm about to cumm! Ooh I'macum…" Sara moans as she rubs the dick against the side of her face and pushes her pussy against my hungry mouth and darting tongue. Knowing I was about to help Sara release a well built up nut motivated me as I treated her clit like a speed bag.

"Ahhhhhh!" That was Sara's response to the great head I was giving her.

I slowly and lightly trace my hard clit with my finger as I look up at Sara as she work a condom on the dick sticking out the hole. Damn, I hate that I need this, but just the thought of that big black dick rubbing against my pussy walls and those strong hands gripping my waist had my pussy vibrating.

With the condom on Sara and I switch positions. I straddle Sara in a 69 with my ass facing the dick. Shaking with anticipation as Sara reaches between my legs and place the dick in position. Feeling the heat from my pussy instinctively the hands grab my hips and guide me.

"Oh, ahh, ahhhhh." To cut off my moans I attack Sara's pussy, sucking on her clit like a thumb. Catching the rhythm Sara finds her way to my clit and that's when things got crazy for me…

CHAPTER 3

"Where the money lil BITCH!" Officer Berry asks the young hustler who he had face down on the alley ground off Livernois.

"Man I ain't got no money!" Berry looked at his partner who takes his eyes from the busy street to step on the hustler's hand, grinding hard.

"Ahhhhh SHIT! Get off my hand!"

"When he do you reach in yo pockets, yo ass, or wherever and you better come out with some money," Berry says giving his partner a nod. After getting his hand free the hustler begins struggling. Berry hit him with two body shots while yelling at him to stop struggling.

"I ain't struggling! Okay, okay… I'm getting the money!" The young nigga pleaded breathing hard and in pain.

Putting the money in his pocket Berry lifts the hustler to his feet just as a white blazer backs into the alley entrance blocking the way. Officer Conley instantly draws his pistol not willing to take no chances. On the streets of Detroit it's not far fetch to hear about two cops being found dead in an alley. Berry holds the hustler in front of him like a shield. Moose hops out of the passenger side of the SUV in a black ball cap cocked to the side with 'POLICE' written across the front in red. Dressed in a black tee, jeans, and Timberlands with a chrome pistol on her hip.

Still not holstering his pistol Conley looks to the driver side as Tots steps out, standing 5'6" and 145 lbs. Tots is one of them females you see from the front and assume from her hips and thighs that she'll have a fat ass, but she don't. Walking toward Conley in a white hoodie with her hands in her hoodie pockets she in blue jeans and shell toes, smiling. Tots takes the chain out that she keeps around her neck with her detective badge on it and lets it fall on her chest. Closing the distance accompanying Moose, still smiling Tots looks back and forth between the cops.

"What's going on?"

"Police business," Conley says as he holsters his pistol, irritation dripping from every word.

"Bitch nigga!" Moose says as she takes a step towards him.

"Chill Mo," Tots says stopping her with her arm. "Hus, they take something off you?" Tots asks the young nigga.

"Fuck yeah! These bitches took $2,500 from me!"

Tots whistles… "That's a come up."

"Fuck outta here," Berry says as he slaps the young nigga in the head.

"Tots, you see the numbers on these pig's whip?"

"Yes sirrr!" Tots responds with her arms folded.

"Those eastside numbers," Moose says.

"So why is an eastside patrol team shaking down on Livernois?" Tots shoots out there.

"You want him? Here," Berry says pushing the hustler toward Moose. "Come on Conley."

"Whoa, whoa! Conley? Berry?" Tots says pointing at each one. Both cops look surprised.

"Don't look surprised… Now hand me the money and I won't report you." Tots said as she reached her hand out in the universal sign (give it here). Berry looks pissed as he reaches in his pocket and pulls out the wad of cash and hands it to Moose.

"Fuckin' bitches," he mumbles.

"Yeah and you just got robbed by two bitches, Pig!" Moose tells him as they stare each other down. Conley grabs at Berry trying to pull him away knowing his partner, knocking Moose out was possible.

Not taking her eyes off Berry Moose raised the money and counted out two hundred and handed it to the hustler.

"What the fuck detective Moose, Tots? Don't I get my gwap back?" Anger and hurt in the young nigga's voice… "Come on that wasn't the deal."

Tots turns her back and threw up the deuces leaving both the cops and the little nigga fuming. The back of her sweater reading:

PO-PO
FIVE-O
TWELVE
THEM BITCHES!!!

"Rich Tony called, I told him that you'll have that info for him tonight," Joyce tells me this as I fly down Livernois.

"So you going to tell me what Bennie said or what?" I love Joyce. She was once my 3rd grade teacher, now my secretary who watches too many cops movies.

"Well is this line… you know, secure?" Joyce asks in a whisper. See what I'm saying? It takes more than I have not to laugh at her when she does shit like this. Not wanting to encourage her I fake like she's irritating me and scream on her…

Seeing police lights in my rearview I get the info from Joyce and end the call as I pull over.

"Turn the vehicle off and step out of the car nigga bitch!" Hearing Tots voice on the intercom I turn MoneyBaggs back up to the max and step out the car. Giving Tots and Moose the finger and grabbing my pussy as I recite Baggs.

"I got scars on my feet/ from kicking doors and robberies."

Just as I reach my trunk they both step out of the Blazer. It's a good thing I got fucked good because if I sat on this trunk earlier my pussy would've been going crazy from the vibration, I think as I watch my fine-ass best friend Tots still rocking the Halle Berry do she wore in high school. No, we never fucked around or even came close, but I would. Shid! She so fuckin' fine. She has the same complexion as me and she got a sexy-ass smile that go crazy with them high cheek bones. But it's her walk that's crazy, and Tots knows it. Super model like, so different from my duck walk!

"What up PIGS!"

"Fuck you, Bitch!" they both say in sync, a testament to all the time they spend together as partners.

"Where y'all headed?"

"This hoe," Moose says pointing at Tots, "got us on the Mayor detail." Moose said joining me on my trunk.

"Bitch you still fuckin' Church?" I asked shocked.

"Uhh yeah, sometimes."

"I told the bitch she fuckin' the wrong one. She should be fuckin' Ebony." Moose says rubbing her thighs looking like a fiend.

"Eww! Naw I'll leave that to y'all." Hearing Ebony's name had me having flashbacks like a muthafucka. Not even Moose and Tots knew about my high school crush...

"GODDAMN!" Moose yells jumping off the trunk. "That muthafucka got my dick jumping and you just sitting there like that, Vegas?"

Moose cuff her pussy, causing me and Tots to fall out laughing at her animated ass.

"Nigga, I'm 30 minutes from 3 nuts so I'm cool, Huh!"...

I chop it up with them for a minute talking shit making sure we was still on for watching the game at my house tomorrow.

"Okay, I'm out. I got real work to do... Real work," I aim the last part at Tots before I spin off giving them the finger.

Later on that evening after a light day closing a case from last week. Last week some niggas hit up the owners of a corner store as they were coming out after closing for $200,000. The owners paid me fifty thousand to find out who did it. Before he hired me of course I knew who did it already. I wouldn't be me if I didn't. So I had Spokes call the niggas anonymously telling them to pay $20,000 to keep his mouth shut. So for the last week I have been working the case waiting to see if these niggas going to play ball or not. Let's just say it's not the first time my info got some niggas killed... "Yeah, a light day." I say as I walk into The Holy Water, a.k.a. Rev's. In the dim light I see Rev behind the bar, his salt and pepper hair twisted in two braids reaching the middle of his back. With his wrinkle-free clean-shaved golden face it's hard to believe he's 50 now. Due to his native heritage some people call him Chief. Due to him in his younger days selling dope out of a church those who know him most intimate call him Rev.

"Rev!" I yell and get no response. I try again. "Rev!" Knowing that I was getting ignored on purpose didn't stop me from being pissed. Since I been back he stopped answering to me calling him Rev.

"Pops!" He turned around and gave me a wink. I promised myself to get him back before the night is over. Excusing himself from a customer Rev approached me with his arms wide still smiling. Standing 6'3" I half hug him and give him a love tap on the kidney. Since I was 6 Rev had me and Moose in boxing and self-defense classes.

"You put yo hands on an old man like that?"

"Nigga you ain't that old, you still bussing Joyce down." Rev chuckles hard before he responds.

"Yeah I still do my thing." Shaking his head and quickly throwing a left jab that I block with my shoulder and hold the phone on the hook that came next before catching him with a love tap to his mid-section.

"Alright, alright!" He yells jumping back to avoid another tap. "Come have a drink wit yo old man, then you can ask me about the backroom. What you having D'Usse?" Rev asks as he moves behind the bar.

"Nah, Vodka." I say and stop, making sure I don't get too close to the other customers. Not everybody knows about the backroom and I'd hate for the wrong person to hear. Not that anything crazy that I can't handle might go down, but it will be fucked up if the police ran in here.

"So how many people back there?"

"15-20." Rev says before downing his whiskey.

"What you didn't count?" I hate walking back there not knowing how many people are back there. "Who patted them down, Seven?" Already knowing the answer but I was light weight pissed.

"Calm down... that's your business back there and I don't work for you. Hire somebody to worry about that shit you asking! Now Vegas beat your feet, before I prove you right that I'm not old!" Rev calmly snaps at me.

I was happy that I irritated him, "Old nigga you ain't ready!" I tell him smiling as I shadow box my way to the back room.

Once a barber college before Rev bought it and turned it into this bar and built an apartment above it. He let me knock down all the walls in the back to a very spacious room plus a comfortable office.

I walked into a thick cloud of weed smoke as I stepped through the door, not seeing Seven but feeling his presence to my right. Before taking another step I smile at the ex-con, standing 6'1" and 260 lbs solid. At first I just gave him a job while he was on papers fresh out of jail, trying to look out. I had him doing little shit like play bodyguard when I was out on bullshit. I figured I'll let him take the first bullets as I get the fuck out the way, but once I opened this up I figured he'll do good at this. Shit, he didn't have nothing else going on. Still not taking a step further I scan the room taking note of the full five tables in my little gambling house.

Today was all cards night and seeing most of the same gamblers as usual I relax a little. First looking at the money table instantly I'm not liking what I see on Brittany's face. People start to notice me as I move deeper into the room and start to yell. "HOUSE!"

Ignoring the gamblers I make eye contact with all my dealers trying to pick up the vibe. Liking what I see I continue to my office noticing only 4 females working the floor and not 6. I like to make it known that I do not sell pussy. I don't take money from women or men for what they do sexually. But I do know niggas will play boss in front of bad bitches. So I keep 6 bad bitches around and if a nigga want to pay for something he like, FUCK IT! But ain't shit free!

Tricks rushes me when I step into my office, "Ooh my baby!" I love my greyhound. Going to one knee I bear hug her. I remember how my cop friends clowned me when I brought Tricks around. I won Tricks from a dog fight. Her old owner used to chain her up when she was in heat with her ass faced out. Then he would let his fighting dogs take turns in the room. Every time I think about that I wish I would've shot him instead of making a bet that Scar would beat two of his dogs at once. That night I won 5 grand. Tricks and I got to kill two of his dogs.

"Jssiah, what's poppin' blood?" I speak into the phone as I light a blunt, my first today since I don't smoke 'til I knew for sure I'm done working for the day.

"Vegas, what up doh!" Sounding like he was doing the same thing I'm doing I think as I inhale on the blunt.

"You tell me, I know you got a show coming up in the city. Where you at now?" Jssiah is a well-known rapper from Detroit, me and him go way back, all the way back to when I was undercover and we kicked in a few doors.

"Shit, I'm in Chicago, baby. What up, you want some tickets? Because Detroit my city, I don't need security." Jssiah chuckles after saying this. Everybody know I take people saying shit like that as disrespect. Not knowing it but he just caused himself to get taxed!

"Nigga, you tried it. But for real, if this was yo city and not mines. Well tell me." Since I like the drama I pause to inhale on my blunt. "Tell me how I know you in the city?" I blew the smoke into the speaker. Jssiah can't help but laugh, not knowing how deep shit was about to get for him.

"Okay, put me in the loop."

"Well I know you in the southwest…"

"Man, what the fuck! You watching me!" Jssiah screams.

"Stop it. I told you this my city."

See, niggas say this they city thinking because they was born here or they getting money here they can claim that title. I tell these niggas this Tat on my head is not for fashion. It's a fore warning, that if you do it here then I'm going to know about it!

"Now I know two more things. One, I know you over there picking up 20 bricks of Boy and 9 bricks of Fetty."

"Come on, these boys over here ratting?"

"Naw, if they was I wouldn't be able to help you. Is they done packing yo stash spot? The one you got in yo tour bus roof?" After that line I sit back and smile. I love fuckin' up his mind like this. When these niggas gonna learn never let a nigga make your stash spot if you plan to buy or sell work in that city and to use stolen license plates after that and get a new paint job.

I allow Jssiah to vent knowing how polished he thinks he is. Hearing me tell him about his shit like that for sure was getting somebody killed tonight.

"Okay, I'm cool. Tell me how much it's gonna cost me?"

"60 G's and a brick a piece."

"Wheew! Come on Vegas, we go too far back for that… Who got you out that East Warren shit?" Jssiah asks.

"Yeah, but not before you let them niggas hit me wit those buck shots!" I gotta chuckle a little thinking about us. Well, really just me standing there with one of his homies dead at my feet and surrounded by 6 trigger happy killers.

"Vegas, come on… even though that nigga you killed was a rat you do remember you was a cop at the time. I had to make it look good." We both knew I was far from a cop at anytime and that's why he fucked with me, but I'm going to let that slide.

"Okay it's a go, fuck wit me."

"You got the narcs waiting on all the freeways for your tour bus, and you got them Dexter boys on you line, the shoot first kind, about 6 to 8 of them linking up on the street ready to light yo ass up!" I tell Jssiah this but not that I'm the reason for the niggas on his ass.

"So what's the plan? I know I'm not paying just for that info. You gotta be getting me outta here and the city!"

I lay it out for Jssiah easy and he tells me my shit will be at Chef's in an hour... "Easy money!"

Wondering if I'm going to be paying bond or funeral charges for the 6 niggas was holding space in my head as I sit at the money table. Steaming thinking how Brittany let this nigga Moon go up $50,000! Looking at the other table and they were all up. The spade table, Charlie and Tasia are up $11,000, Tonk's table up 3 g's and both the Omaha tables up 5-6 grand a piece. Just the money table, where I sit now, is the only table where you have to have $25,000 to get a seat at the Texas Hold 'Em table. Every table holds 5 seats not including the dealer. To step back here costs, and most times all other shit happens back here. Also, for some this is a safe place to conduct all kinds of business.

Showing his gap fronts Moon sits across from me smiling. Rich Tony's fat ass sits to my left gassing him up.

"Moon brought the real house out ta'night!"

"Yeah, Rich they say Vegas never loses. It's gon lose ta'night!" Moon says causing the table to burst out laughing. Everybody but me as I pick up my hand and see I got Queen/9 suited (hearts).

Rich Tony bet fifteen hundred. Freaky takes his time as usual...

"Freak, what you got over there, five thousand? Man throw that little shit in there!" Brick shoot at Freaky. He being from PA and Freaky being from 7 mile so they always throwing shots at each other.

"You might as well Freak, you done blew yo re-up already!" I join in trying to build the pot up. I was feeling my hand. Usually I'm right. Never have I closed them doors even or down, I wasn't about to let this gap-toothed nigga come in here and come up. Plus Brittany told me the nigga didn't even have all the money to come through them doors. I take so much from these niggas I let them slide once in a while. But never will I let a nigga like Moon leave up fifty grand.

"What Vegas... I'm from 7 mile!" Freaky screams standing up and pulling out two big ass knots and throwing down on the table.

"Tracy, bring this nigga some mo chips!" Brick yells. Being used to these niggas clowning each other Tracy doesn't even look this way.

Anxious to see the flop I ask Freaky again is he calling or folding?

"Fuck it, I fold!"

"7 mile niggas stay faking," Moon says as he raises the bet to three bands. Eastside Rick calls and so does Brick. I call and turn the flop over. A 10 and 9 of spades and a queen of diamonds show... Damn why those couldn't be hearts? Bitch cause you got the queen and 9 of hearts, I say to myself and chuckle on the inside.

Rich Tony don't waste no time, he instantly folds. Moon stares me down still smiling.

"I bet a red chip."

Eastside Rick folds leaving me and Brick to call or fold.

"Fuck it, I call." Brick says sounding like he knew it was a bad call. Hands down I know Moon got the flush draw. But what the fuck do this nigga Brick got? Probably tripps, I gotta get this nigga out the way. I'm either going to beat Moon head up or lose and have this nigga robbed later.

"You know what? I call yo 10 bands and raise you 20 mo!"

"Man, what the fuck!" Brick shouts, pissed he was caught in the bet.

"What? I thought y'all PA niggas was racked up? I call." Moon says as he throws his chips in.

"Fuck it, I'm down anyways. I'm all in with that." Brick says standing up behind his chair. I flip over the turn and it's a 3 of spades.

"Oh! I'm all in 45 bands!" Moon quickly says after seeing the card.

"That's right buss her ass Moon!" Freaky says giving Moon the 7 mile hand shake.

"Fuck around and break the bank ta'night!" Moon yells getting everybody's attention...

Loving the drama I call Tracy over. "Bring me my bitch," I tell her, referring to my naked female weed pipe.

"Man I don't think she looked at her hand at all dawg." Brick says, and I haven't since the flop. That's my thing I look at it once and make sure I put it to the side and never touch it again. Niggas never know if I'm on some bullshit or not.

"Man, fuck that! What's up House?" Moon asks me.

"Calm down." I say as I stuff my bitch's ass. Already knowing I'm calling since I made my mind up on robbing Moon if I lose to him. I take a deep pull as I rub Trick's head.

"You know what?" ...exhale... "I'm feeling that's my card." I throw my chips in the pile. Moon flip over his cards showing the ace and 5 of spades.

Just as I thought, I think as I flip over the River and it's a queen of clubs... Whew! I don't know how I stayed calm knowing how bad I wanted to smack that smile off of Moon's face.

"OH SHIT!" Brick yells flipping over his pocket 9's.

"OOH!" Rich Tony and Freaky yell.

"That's cool, that's cool. I get the other pot." Moon says as he starts dapping Brick up. Acting confused I ask Brick what he has, pointing out that I see Moon's flush, I gather up the chips.

"Whoa! Whoa!" Moon yells.

"Vegas stop bullshitting... you see I got 9's over queens," Brick says smiling.

"Ohhh! Well that's stupid. You got two hands what you need three 9's for?" I pick up my cards and throw them on the table face up. "I rather have three bitches and two 9's," I say chuckling.

Sitting back in my office with my feet up I hand Rich Tony my phone.

"You fucked Moon up on that table for real." He says as he looks through the pictures of Buff coming out of a hotel. A few days ago Buff supposedly robbed Rich Tony's stash house for 12,000 pills and somehow he robbed the plug for the money Rich Tony just paid catching him before crossing the bridge back to Canada. So he hired me to find Buff within 5 days. One thing for sure that bag gonna be short some bands and pills.

"And you say you found him where?"

"He in Ink town."

"You know if he got my shit still? Because at the end of the day I need that and who helped his bitch ass rob me!"

"I'll have to assume he still got yo shit. But I got somebody watching him and as far as I know he ain't been nowhere."

CHAPTER 4

Damn it feels good out here. Another sunny day. I made so much money yesterday I might go buy some shit for my loft. Dressed in blue jeans and a white V neck that's stretched to the tee trying to contain my cups. My number ten Jordan's and my Detroit Snap Back on backwards with my two pistols hanging as usual. I was feeling good today walking from Rev's to the Coney just down the street on Grand River.

"Vegas! Vegas!" Hearing my name I turn towards the voice while reaching for a pistol. Hand on the butt I see it's Highway Man who's calling me as he dodges cars coming my way.

"Pss..." What the fuck he want? Looking like a man who woke up in a cardboard box. Feigning, Highway Man gets straight to the point when he reach me finally.

"Vegas, Vegas, I got some info just for you." Highway Man says looking like he's in pain.

"I'm cool, now get the fuck out of my face!" Not hiding my irritation at all. That's how you got to be with these fuckers or every chance they get they'll be bringing you bullshit! Turning to walk away this muthafucka grabs my elbow. I snatch my shit away and side kick this nigga in the knee causing him to fall to his other knee screaming.

"What the fuck! AHH!" He screams as I dig my hands deep into his shoulder.

"Next time…" I dig harder.

"Ahhh!"

"Shut the fuck up! Next time I'm going to break your jaw and then yo fingers!" I say before letting him up. But instead Highway Man stays on his knees.

"Come on Vegas, you gonna want to hear dis." Highway Man plead. Liking what I see I ask him how much it's going to cost me.

"I just need some air in my tire. Give me two zeros."

"A hundred dollas! Man I'll give you $10."

"Ten dollas! Man ten dollas ain't get me right since '99, naw they had that shit on the Eastside b."

WHACK!! I smack the shit out of Highway Man causing him to fall to the ground twisting and holding his face. I grab him by his dirty collar.

"Stay focused, I'll give you fifty and if I can use the info I'll give you the other half."

"Okay, listen. Last night I was behind the Big Store wit Bay Bay getting the meat cleaned off my bone, ya know! I kno you heard about Bay Bay. Then out of the blue a Cadillac Van pulls up since I was behind the garbage can."

I was getting tired of Highway Man so I cocked my hand back again as if I was going to knock his head off.

"Okay, okay! That body they pulled from behind there this morning, that was Buff." Highway Man was talking so fast I didn't really catch it so I had him repeat it.

"So Buff got killed last night and?" Really pissed that this nigga thought I'd want to know this.

"Nooo! Vegas, the thing I seen Corn kill him last night." Highway Man had the sense to whisper the last part. But it made sense with Corn being Rich Tony's cousin.

"What time was this?"

"Around one in the morning." That makes sense since I gave Rich that info around 11:00pm.

"Highway Man, get yo simple ass up and if I was you I'd keep my mouth shut about what you seen. Right now I'm thinking about calling Corn up right now!"

"Ooh! Vegas, don't say that… you the only one I told this to! Come on don't do dis to- to me!"

"I'm not. Just take this fifty and get the fuck on."

Now I'm sitting at a table in the Coney with a half-eaten omelet and half a cup of orange juice sitting in front of me as I talk to Joyce. For some strange reason she was on one this morning.

"Joyce, contact Rich Tony. Ask him if that info come through. If he says no send Spokes over to the Coney."

"You should bring your ass into the office! Some lady keep calling here asking for you never staying on the phone long enough to give her name once I tell her you're not in!" I look at my phone thinking Rev must not be laying it down like he think, got Joyce cussing at me like this.

"Fuck her then, Joyce! I'll be in later and get some dick!" I end the call as she's screaming my name.

Man, what I'm going to do with this info? If Rich Tony didn't have his cousin kill Buff then Corn for sure the one who helped Buff rob him. That's really the only way this info is valuable and that's what I'm hoping.

My phone starts vibrating fucking up my train of thought. Not noticing the number I pick up, "Who the fuck is this?"

"Well that's no way to answer the phone, Miss." Annoyed by the woman's proper speech and the 'Miss' shit I end the call…

"Who the fuck is this!" I answer again when the phone vibrates. The lady on the other end chuckles.

"Vegas, this is Cherish Towns. I'm the lieutenant mayor," Cherish says matter-of-factly in her proper way.

"And his Mother-in-law," I shoot back at her.

"Yes, so now that you know who I am will you be more civilized now?"

"Are you the one who been calling my office?" I ask ignoring her question.

"Yes," Cherish says calmly.

"Why?"

"Because I wish to hire you. You are a private investigator, correct?"

"Hump! I guess. So you want to talk over the phone or in person?" I was hoping she would say in person and I was hoping I can get a look at Ebony.

"Come to the Mayor's Mansion 1:00 this afternoon. We should be able to talk then."

Damn, look at this fine-ass chocolate bitch here! Google said she was 52, but Cherish Towns could easily pass for 40 at the most. The first person who came to mind when she looked up from her phone was Gab. That short bob and damn, I can see where Ebony got those cheek bones from. Cherish had the type of thickness that comes with age; Michelle Obama like, far from skinny like her daughter Ebony. But this old bitch is for sure fuckable, so much so that I was getting horny looking at her as I sit on this plush couch waiting on her to end her call. Looking around the mansion I wasn't impressed at all. Shit looked old and expensive...

"So can I get you anything to drink? Water, tea, or something stronger?" I was zoning out so hearing her address me slightly threw me off. She had one of those voices and demeanors Tyler Perry portrays in his movies of a successful black woman.

"Naw, I'm fine."

"Well Vegas, you look different from the young lady that I remember watching play basketball." She says this as she's taking a seat across from me and I'm not sure if she's referring to my scars, piercings, or tattoos. Shit, probably all of it. I chuckle as I shrug my shoulders.

"That's life."

Cherish chuckles. "That's the truth... So let's get to business. I'm a busy woman and I know you probably are too. I want to find out who the Mayor is cheating on my daughter with." The straight way she said this fucked me up a little. Not really knowing what to expect when I came in here, but this was far from my mind.

"Sorry Ms. Towns, but I don't do the… 'follow the cheating husband around' thing." I slowly stand as I'm putting my snapback on, fake leaving knowing after she told this that there was no way she was going to let me leave like this.

"I'll double what you charge!" Cherish says quickly before I could stand straight. Inwardly I'm smiling.

"Do you know what I charge?" I ask with a smile.

"No, but it doesn't matter just send me the bill."

Come on, like I can't see an easy lick. I mean shit I already know who the Mayor is cheating with! I sit my ass right down and played the role!

"What makes you think he's cheating?"

Cherish stands and heads for the mini-bar and pours herself something brown, downing the shot. "It's just something I can feel. Something I just know."

"So why it's you and not Ebony I'm talking to?" Cherish waves me off and I was really confused by her emotions as she went into a list of the suspicious behaviors of a cheating husband which she thought the Mayor was displaying. Still leaving me confused as to why it was her and not Ebony I was talking to… But fuck it! "I need twenty-one hundred to start, and…"

"Deal!" Cherish said, cutting me off.

"Wait what if I come back with nothing?" Which was likely going to happen.

Cherish looked up from her purse, "Then you're not as good as you think." She said it so matter of fact that it made me think she knew who Mayor Church was fuckin' too!

The door opened and to my pleasure Ebony walked in.

"Ma, you ready? We…" Ebony stopped once she saw me.

Just like in high school my eyes darted to Ebony's pussy. I was disappointed, seeing her in a navy blue pencil skirt. That still wasn't stopping me from thinking back to seeing her long slim legs in her cheerleader uniform or in a pair of tight jeans, and that gap made her fat pussy print. Imagining this doesn't make me feel like a pervert, I just like a fat pussy and Ebony was my crush all through my freshman year of high school.

"VEGAS! That's you? Ohmygod!" Ebony screamed rushing toward me with her phone in her hand. I'm shocked not only by how fast she move in those heels, but also her reaction to seeing me. Shit, I'm a playa and I hide my surprise well. I just smile and take her into my arms.

I inhale deeply and whisper, "Damn you smell good," before softly kissing her ear knowing I was taking a chance. It wasn't like we were super close during high school, with Ebony being three grades ahead of me.

"Oh my god, I haven't seen you in so long." Hearing her say that as she steps out of my arms had me thinking she didn't hear me or felt my light kiss. But Ebony pulled me by the hand and back down to sit on the couch beside her. Not letting her hand go I began softly rubbing my thumb up and down Ebony's fingers. I know this bitch can feel this! I heard Tots and Moose's names but I wasn't listening. The only thing on my mind was how can I get Ebony alone. It didn't seem like Cherish was paying attention either, she was back on her phone. That was until Ebony asked, as if it's just hitting her, why I was here. Luckily Cherish was fast on her feet because like always this slim bitch had me gone.

"Well your friend Vegas is a P.I." Cherish said not looking up from her phone, making two things clear to me. One, she was good at lying, and two, that this was clearly her idea alone. Both things were important to know.

"Ohm, that's interesting… Wait, Ma. I know you're not wasting Vegas's time on that missing jewelry." Ebony said turning from me to her mom. Breaking my heart for a second when she withdrew her hand from mine. But lighting a fire in my pussy when she let her hand fall lazily on my thigh. Man, I can't see how Ebony's hand didn't get 3rd degree burns! I know she has to feel the heat coming from my pussy.

"Yeah Ebony, I told you no one can be here working while stealing from us!"

"I see you're going to do as you like no matter what anyone say or feel." Ebony turned back to me as I notice her hand high on my thigh while biting her lip she glance up at me.

"Damn Vegas, I see you still thick. Look at your thigh compared to my little leg!" Ebony says playfully as she gets her feel on while squeezing my thigh with both hands.

"You know what, we should get together and have lunch or something!" Damn she sounded like she was really trying to catch up to an old friend. Shit, the first chance I get to be with her alone I'm diving in head first!

I give Ebony my number. "Don't make me wait too long." I whisper in her ear as I hug her before leaving.

That night I couldn't stop thinking about Ebony, wondering if I read her wrong. Shit nowadays it's hard to find a bitch that don't fuck around. Back in high school, just the thought of Ebony letting me eat her up was laughable, at least to me it was. Now I was reflecting on some of the times we spoke in high school when I was still in the closet and unlike Moose I used to duck the girls' locker room after games. I just never knew how I'd react to being around all that pussy like that. But still Ebony never gave off the vibe like today! Something about her slim ass had me moist all day! Shit! I'm contemplating now if I can rub one out real quick before everybody shows up to watch the basketball game.

Of course just then Moose and Tots come through the door loud AS FUCK!

"I got $500 on the Pistons!" Moose screamed as she ran and leapt over the back of my couch and landed next to me. Fuck!

"Nigga this ain't that cheap shit across the street! Don't jump on my shit like that!" You know I'm pissed these bitches fucked up my moment.

"Damn! Bitch, I thought you got some pussy ta'day?" Tots throws her two cents in coming from my small bar with a fifth of D'Usse and some glasses.

"Vegas, what the fuck!" Moose yells as she picks up the remote. "Why don't you have the pregame show on wit Chuck and them." These hoes always blowing my shit! Then I see Church's bald-headed ass on the screen and I instantly think about why her ass ain't call me yet! Looking at this nigga, bald dark and handsome is how they describe him. Shit, I guess if you into niggas...

"Damn, bitch! All that dick sucking you do you couldn't get us to the game?" Moose says, fake mad.

"Nigga bitch, I don't suck his dick. I leave that to his wife. Plus I could've got us on the detail, but he's not going to be there for the whole game. He and Ebony got some type of dinner to attend." I perk up hearing that at least now I know why she hasn't hit me up. Now that I think about it, should I tell Tots about this case? Even though I have no intentions of revealing their affair... so damn do it really matter if I tell her... fuck it!

"Moose I'll take that bet. Blazers about to put dick all in the Pistons. But we gotta give the money to Rev once he gets her before the game. Can't trust a PIG!"

"BITCH!" Tots and Moose say at the same time before rushing me!

A slight hangover and five hundred dollas short since the Pistons punished the Blazers taking a 3-1 lead in the Championship. I'm back in the Coney with my worker Spokes, while face-timing Joyce.

"Joyce rent me a Malibu and have it parked in front of Rev's. I gotta do some surveillance." Might as well play the part for that two bands, I mean I already know who he fuckin, plus I might come across anything... "Have info come in on Marcus's case, I gotta close that this week." For the past few months some cop been shaking down this nigga Marcus. After he couldn't get the info on the cop on his own, he finally came to me. Tsk tsk... When these niggas gonna learn.

Joyce smack her lips. I guess she been saying something and now she was shaking her head in irritation.

"If you start checking your inbox or if you came in more often you wouldn't be asking these questions." Joyce says before ending the call.

Leaving me stunned as I look from my phone to Spokes with a smirk on my face.

"Damn Boss!" Spokes says to me as he washed down his bacon with some orange juice. Spokes is a 13-year-old 7th grade drop-out. I use him to do all types of odd jobs. He's called 'Spokes' because of his passion for bikes. He builds them, fixes them, and rides them; paddle to motor bikes.

Yesterday I had Spokes deliver a message to Rich Tony then I sent him to break into one of Rich Tony's houses. Hoping Rich Tony takes his cousin there, which he did. Rich Tony probably forgot telling me about his "Blood house" as he calls it, on one of those nights we were sharing stories, drunk.

Let Spokes tell it, Rich Tony and three of his goons dragged Corn into the house legs and arms chained. They took him to the dining room where wooden beams hung across the ceiling above a small tub which Rich Tony and his goons filled with cold water and cement.

"Cuz, what the fuck dis about!" Corn continues to ask as Rich Tony ignores him while sitting in a chair smoking a blunt. One of the goons tied a rope through the chains on Corn's legs and threw the rope through a series of beams hanging from the ceiling.

"Pull his bitch ass up," Rich Tony calmly says.

"Come on Cuz, don't do dis!" Corn yells as tears flow from the corners of his eyes as he hangs upside down above the cement-filled tub.

"Where my shit?"

"Cuz, what shit!"

"Dip him, 10 seconds." Rich Tony raises his arms to indicate for his goon to pull Corn up. Once Corn's head was clear of the tub a goon would come and throw steaming hot water on Corn to clear the cement from his face.

Spokes said they did this twice before Corn told Rich Tony where his pills and money were.

Then Rich Tony told his cousin he hoped he can hold his breath for 3 minutes. Then Rich Tony taped Corn's mouth before they dipped Corn again for what Spokes said felt like a full minute at least. After pulling him back up they turned a fan on to speed up the drying.

"Man, I held my breath the whole time, scared as fuck!" Shit, Spokes still sounded scared as he told me the story.

"Man I don't know when his 3 minutes started cause dat felt like 5 minutes! Vegas, you shouldn't seen it! Corn's face stuck in the cement. His chest was still moving so you know he was alive, but when he stopped shaking that's when I damn near screamed."

Hearing and seeing Spokes made me chuckle.

"Imagine what they would've done to yo little punk ass... So did he make it?"

"Sorry Vegas but I couldn't take it. I got the fuck outta there!" I burst out laughing! Embarrassing the fuck out of Spokes but I couldn't help it.

"It's cool. Nah, for real it's cool Spokes. And I'm gonna give you all yo paper too."

Damn, I should've gotten Ebony's number! Man, you'd think I never had pussy the way this bitch got me. Look at me... I keep going through my phone and shit...

Damn whoever coming my way is walking hard as fuck in them heels. I think as I hear footsteps. It's evident that this bitch wants some attention. I'm just going to keep my head down and pray she goes past me. As the footsteps get closer of course I take a peek. I see black ugly toes with red nail polish sticking out of some expensive leather strapped heels stopping at the seat that Spokes just abandoned.

"Excuse me, Vegas." DAMN! I heard of women with deep voices or studs trying to make their voices sound deeper, but this was a deep voice trying to sound like a woman's and it just wasn't working! Man I really don't want to see the person this voice belongs to. Slowly I take in what's in front of me.

Standing in a pair of tight Prada jeans and basing off the legs and thighs alone this was a running back in front of me. Believe me, I don't want to see this so I'm taking my time on purpose. No hips and a waist that only could be designed by a doctor. Looking at the print in my face even though I knew before that this was a nigga, I really knew now. Completing my analysis of the lower part I had to see this person. The first thing that crossed my mind once I met his eyes was, 'poor doctor!' This person had one of the strongest faces I have ever seen on a tranny. Whatever he was trying to accomplish he failed. This dude was ugly! Only thing that was good about it was that he didn't have a beard. He looked kind of familiar, but without a doubt I have never met this person.

"Who the fuck is you?" I ask as I sit back and then I notice the two guys with him.

"Flex." The man says as he extends his hand.

I nod. "Flex, take a seat. I don't like dick in my face... Those some nice titties you got there." I wasn't lying about that. His shit really was sitting up nice.

"Yeah girl, they better!" Flex says looking down at his C-cups.

"Where you from Flex?" You can tell he was from the South even though his accent wasn't thick.

"I'm from here but I been in the 'A' for a couple years now... Can't you tell?" Smiling with two stud diamonds in both nostrils and a loop in his bottom lip. Whereas I got stud diamond middle fingers in my ears, Flex had several earring loops and studs in both ears.

Taking all this in I was itching to get this thing out of my face. Already I wasn't doing business with him.

"So what made you come in here and fuck up my morning?"

"Since this being yo city I figure if anybody can help me... you can." Flex says smiling again. You know you're ugly when your smile makes you uglier! I hope he didn't think by him acknowledging the City as mines that he was sweetening me up. I was now wondering how he found out about me.

Flex whispered something to one of his guys in the booth behind him.

"Help! Shit... my help cost money you gotta know that!" Man, staring at them titties stretching that Prada halter top I can't help but think about how fat this nigga had to be to get titties that size and perfect.

"I got the paper, Ma, but you gotta find my…"

"WHOA! WHOA! Before you say anything else it's going to cost you a ban for me just to listen." Never having been one to pass up on a free ban. Plus, I didn't like this nigga already. So I took my shot plus this will tell me how desperate he is.

"WHAT?... Them yo O.T. prices huh?" I shrug my shoulders before taking a sup of my orange juice. Flex took a sip from his water one of his guy just brought back.

I wonder what type of niggas they were. Shaking my head.

"Come on Vegas, wearing heels and having titties don't make me bitch." Flex said matter-of-factly.

I had to chuckle at that… "Shi-it, paying me a ban don't make you a bitch Flex… but those heels and those (pointing at his chest) FoSho make you a bitch!" His guys stand up after I say that.

"If y'all about to leave take him with you," I say as I look toward Flex ready to snatch my pistols out if he gave the wrong signal…

"Fuck it, what's yo Cash App?"

"Easy Money."

"Gee shoot her the paper. Now, can we talk?"

I nod my head thinking how easy it is to get money out of people these days… Flex hands me his phone as he talks. "That's my niece. She ran away like what…" looking at Gee, "4 ta 5 weeks ago." The girl on the phone looked like she was about 16 going on 25. Every picture on her Instagram she was half-naked with a bottle in her hand. Flex did sound concerned, I'll give him that, and I see why. Little bitch was asking for something to happen to her.

"Ran away from where?"

"Atlanta."

"How long she been in the City?" Going through her pictures I didn't see nothing to tell me she was here.

"She only been in the 'D' for about 10 days. We been following her trying to catch her." Flex shrugs his shoulders and I'm noticing his actions don't match up with the concern in his voice.

"I see the last time she posted something was 3 days ago. How old is she, 16 and posting pictures like this…" I say out loud before handing the phone back to Flex. "So why is she running from you?"

"She 16, Vegas. You know how girls that age are." Once again he didn't look as concerned as he was trying to sound. I really wasn't liking his answers or the idea of this nigga chasing this girl down.

"So you want me to find her and bring her to you or just tell you where she's at?" Flex pause as if in thought…

"How about you find her and then just call me and I'll take it from there."

"I can do that." Hoping I sounded convincing since I had no intentions of delivering this girl to this thing in front of me.

"Well, send me her social media info, two stacks, and I'll get started ASAP!"

Flex chuckled. "Come on Vegas, play fair! We supposed to be LGBT fam."

"Stop right there. I don't fuck with them clowns!" Nigga don't know how much he just pissed me off! "Yeah I'm more Malcolm X and they more MLK! So send me the two bans. If it's going to be a problem paying me you should be leaving!"

"Say no more. Gee, shoot her the bread." Flex said as he stood up and I give him my cell number.

"A, what's her name?" I shout before Flex could get out the door.

"Katrina, but everyone calls her Kitty." Kitty huh? And you wonder why she on social media looking like that, I think, watching Flex and his guys hop into a blue Caddy truck. I went to the counter and got a plastic bag. Bagging up Flex's glass with plans to find out who this nigga really was. Just as I was placing the glass in my trunk my cell goes off and to my delight it was Ebony!

Before going into the Mansion I took my braid out with thoughts of Ebony's hands gripping my shit! Now sitting here in another room inside of this big-ass house waiting as a maid set the table up for what I hope to be a make-believe lunch date.

"The First Lady will be in soon. She said make yourself comfortable." Looking around I notice this room was more cozier than the last room I was in. Along with the couch I was sitting on there were three more with two more tables besides the one in front of me. Across from me on the other side of the table was a leather Lay-Z Boy. I was making real plans on having Ebony on every couch and chair in this room. Damn! Just the thought that I was finally going to get my mouth on her had my mouth watery and dry, how was that possible… Shaking my head I pick up the lemonade and take a big sip.

Ebony stepped into the room and immediately froze me with my glass in my hand as I watched her walk toward me. Comparing her to her younger self I couldn't help but like what I saw, nothing had changed in her figure or look. Ebony still looked like my celebrity crush Kimberly Elise, those cheek bones and those damn lips! Dressed in a burgundy sports bra and maybe I'm tripping or fiening, because with every step she took I swore her nipples on her A-cups were getting harder. By the time Ebony was standing in front of me I was breathing a little faster seeing and feeling the sexual tension in her eyes. My nipples were begging to be released from this sports bra prison and this tight ass Nike shirt I had on.

"Isn't this what you was looking for last time you were here?" Ebony calmly asked with her pussy inches from my nose. "Back in high school I used to catch you checking for my pussy print." Hearing her say she was hip to me was turning me on that and what I was seeing in front of me. Standing in a pair of burgundy leggings Ebony clearly wasn't wearing panties, I don't know how I kept myself from licking or kissing her pussy so far. I inhaled deeply… Ebony natural scent was strong overpowering her expensive perfume.

Downing the rest of my iced lemonade I put the glass down and took hold of her slim hips leaning in I lightly blew my cool breath on Ebony's pussy as I rubbed up and down her thighs.

"Mmmm..." Ebony cooed and slightly shiver, damn she was so sexy! Taking my hands she place them on her little bubble butt and start playing in my hair.

"These scars fit you, I always thought you were too fine to have the demeanor you had."

"Damn Ebony you smell so good... I been thinking about you all day." No longer been able to stop myself I kiss her pussy before letting my tongue rest in the folds of her pussy and taking a deep lick...

"Damn that feel soooo good." Ebony whisper before stepping out of my embrace. FUCK, she tasted so good that area in her leggings was full of her juices and her fat pussy was very visible I notice as she walked backwards to the Lay-Z Boy. Hanging one leg over the arm of the chair Ebony stuff her hands in her leggings slowly working herself. Moaning the whole time while telling me how wet her pussy was and how she was playing with her pussy all yesterday informing me she was just doing that before coming in here. She had me on fire and I could feel my juices dropping out of my pussy running down my leg as I stood up on shaky legs. I took my holster and Nike shirt off in like one motion, my nipple was as hard as they ever been I think.

"Ahhh! Vegas your scars turn me on." Cried Ebony rubbing her clit faster... SHI-T, if scars turned her on like that! I kicked off my Nine-Five's so fast pulling my joggers down instantly letting her see more of my scars.

"Vegas look how wet you are." She say seeing the big wet stain in front of my green cotton panties my pussy clutching that area. Ebony pulled her glistening fingers out of her panties slowly ease them into her mouth...

"Umm..." Ebony moaned as she pulled them out.

"You got to come taste this Vegas I promise you'll never taste nothing this good again." WHAT! I walked over to Ebony taking my time loving the look in her eyes like she couldn't wait to have my lips on her.

Once in front of Ebony I take her hand and slide it in my panties from the side. DAMN! My knees buckle a little when she rubbed my clit and she drove me crazy when she pulled my panties to the side to dip a finger in my hungry pussy. Having to get my hands on my nipples I take off my sports bra, Ebony suck in a breath once she saw my beautiful light brown B-cups. Standing Ebony wipe my juices across my breast then licks the juices off, pinching, licking and sucking my nipples…

    Taking her face in my hands I kiss her passionately. Finally getting my mouth on those sexy lips was a dream come true the taste of both our pussies on her tongue was like a exotic drink. When I pulled Ebony bra off my pussy got a little wetter seeing her huge dark nipples standing a inch off her little titties was a beautiful sight. Tweaking and pulling one nipple I place the other in my mouth and go to work on it.

    "Yesss, ahh unhuh oohh… I like that Vegas, ummm!" Ebony moaned, she was on fire begging for more. I ease my hand in her leggings pulling them down as I fall to my knees, damn her pussy was beautiful. Two perfect tone lip, puffy and dripping. Maybe drunk off lust but I think her pussy spoke to me before I spread her lips and tasted the sweetest pussy I ever came across.

CHAPTER 5

    My office sits on a block by itself across from an abandoned public park so I always park my car a block away which is full of houses and broke down cars lining the curb. It's not unusual to see people since people do live on this side, but seeing a young nigga coming from the block my office is on… now that's reason to pause. I was instantly on my P's and Q's plus I could see a Kevlar police issue bullet proof vest he was wearing under his shirt. Now 5 feet apart from each other the young nigga up his pistol stopping me in my tracks, I was definitely slipping.
    "Bitch! Put yo hands out and walk toward me."
    "Damn, what the fuck!" I should charge this little nigga. I doubt he can fuck with me with the hands.
    "If you even think about reaching for those I'm gon empty yo shit Vegas!"
    For sure I was believing the shooter, this was Detroit. Why the young nigga was talking and not shooting already was shocking. I kept my hands and my thoughts from my pistols while walking towards him. Once in reach the shooter took my arm and pushed his 40.cal in my side. That's where he fucked up! Quickly I snatch

my arm away and lock his gun hand to my side just as the gun was going off.

"DAMN! FUCK!" I yell feeling the heat from the bullet. Knowing I couldn't worry about that now I punch the shooter in the nose then I pushed the locked arm at the elbow upwards. Hearing the arm break I feel the shooter's arm go limp as he threw a wild punch and screamed in pain!

Still a block away and happy no one else was out on the street it was only like two in the afternoon. I punched him in the stomach and I notice the fight was out of the young shooter. I guess the pain from the broken arm and nose was too much. I was hearing him struggle for breath. I pushed him up against the abandoned car, thinking on getting some answers. Getting shot at wasn't new but getting shot out the blue was. I looked up and I saw a black Tahoe coming down the street creeping. I thought it was because I looked strange, until a man hopped out of the back seat with a Draco and let loose!

"OH SHIT!!!" Bullets were flying, knocking metal off the cars that lined the curb.

Not knowing if both shooters were together or not I turned the little nigga around and used him as a shield. Instantly a hollow took off half of his head. Trying to drag the dead weight and keep it upright as I continue to back up and stay shielded by the cars was difficult. With bullets flying like this I knew it was only a matter of time until I was hit and when I was it would be hell. A bullet caught me just a few inches above where the young nigga shot me, more like grazed me.

It sent the type of pain that steals your voice, forming a silent scream, taking the little strength I had left in me making me stumble to the ground and my human shield falling on top of me. Luck was on my side because the shooter was now reloading giving me time to catch my breath and think...

Placing the dead man on my feet and bringing my legs to my chest like I was doing leg presses... One... Two... "Three!" I yell and with all my strength in my legs I push the dead body in the air and quickly bear crawl in the opposite direction. The gunman unloads half his clip in the dead body.

I was 5 cars down now, I pulled out my two babies and hopped from behind the cars and into the street blazing! Catching the gunman off guard I hit him twice, once in the shoulder and once in the hip... As the gunman went down he blindly shoot in my direction. The Tahoe came forward and slightly blocked me as I continued shooting, seeing my bullets bounce off the truck... The gunman limped to the backseat and the SUV sped toward me as I ducked back behind the cars.

Now in my office I lay back in my sports bra as Joyce tends to my wounds. Crazy not even an hour ago I was in my bra about to get some pussy, now look at me!

"I just knew that was you out there when I heard them shots... I called the police."

"Sss! Yeah, me too." I say, obviously in pain.

"You lucky one of them bullets went straight through and the other one only grazed you!"

"Uh-huh!" Going through the young nigga's pockets didn't turn up shit. And no matter how much I rack my brain I couldn't think of anybody who'll come at me like this if I'm looking at it like they were together. If I look at it like two different muthafuckas on my line... WHEW! Oh my god my head instantly started to pound.

As Joyce plays mother bear my mind is going in circles with these thoughts and all the while I was trying to convince Joyce to go home and stay there. Being shot at near the office was a clear warning that she was in danger also. I was closing the office down for a couple of days until I can figure out what's going on, why muthafuckas was trying to wipe me out. It took forever but Joyce gave in so that was one less person I'll have to worry about.

After an hour and a half of rest and two pills I was back in my Charger feeling good flying down the freeway. Seeing Highway Man I pull over and wait by the ramp...

"Highway Man, come take a ride with me," I tell him while I lean up against my car. Highway Man was looking nervous.

"Nah! I'm cooling, Vegas." He says stopping before he reached my trunk.

Not thinking anything's wrong with Highway Man's behavior because this is how he usually is, but I wasn't in the mood for his shit now!

"Man get the fuck in the car and take a ride wit me! As a matter of fact I'll give you the other 50 I owe from earlier." Knowing that would get his attention, I pull out the bill and hand it to him. Wasting no time Highway Man steps up and snatches the 50 from me. Reflexes makes me draw back to knock his fronts out, forgetting my wounds 'til that point! Biting my lip just to stop from screaming.

"My bad! My bad, Vegas!" Highway Man took a step back as he stuffed the money in his pocket. Remembering I needed him I raised my hand and took a deep breath trying to calm myself and ease the pain I was feeling. I was hoping the pills would have a stronger effect soon!

"Highway Man, it's cool, but I'm going to need you to drive. I just popped two pills and I can barely stay awake…" Lying!

Like always, my Charger turned down my block slowly, coaching Highway Man from the passenger seat. I was tilted back with my tinted windows up. I routinely scan the streets. Unlike most Detroit streets I made sure all the streetlights on my block always work. So far I wasn't seeing anything unusual. Like most warm nights people are out socializing, there weren't many, but more than I would like. Passing my house I see Scar walking the yard like a C.O. at count. With all these people out, Scar usually plays the front gate so him not doing that was the first give away something was up. I had Highway Man continue to creep not knowing if he knew where I stayed or not. At the corner I told him to creep into the alley.

There are only three ways into my garage and the alley is the safest for a stranger. Whoever was in my backyard didn't know that and that's what I was counting on. I hop outta my car two houses down while using my garage opener to open my garage door as Highway Man continue to creep down the alley. I'm sure he was thinking I was strange, but if he knew how much danger I was putting him in he'd shit his pants... Actually I was hoping he still would.

With both of my pistols drawn, I wasn't taking no chance not knowing how many people I was dealing with. I put my back to the garage as the car turned into the garage I peel from the alley. Once he turned the car off a nigga with no mask and a big ass pistol rushed in from my backyard. By coming in that way he caused a bucket to topple over from above the frame. At least the nigga was smart enough to wait until the car was off before busting in and blazing.

Either not caring or for some strange reason not smelling the gasoline that just spilled on him the shooter continued to let loose despite the bullets ricocheting off my bulletproof Charger. I put my pistols away, hearing Highway Man screaming really had me wanting to stay in hiding. Just as I was revealing myself with match in hand the shooter got too close to the sparks from the ricocheting bullets. Fire leaped on his chest. He was screaming instantly before the flame engulfed his whole body... I seen the fire spreading on the floor and the walls of my garage behind the shooter as he stumble toward me. Stepping to the side tripping the shooter as I go pick up the fire extinguisher that I keep in the garage. Pulling out my phone I call the cops while standing over the burning body, finally Highway Man comes out of the car visibly shaking.

"Whaaaa what da fuck!" He yells at me as I'm putting the fire out on the burning body. Not saying a word I turn the fire extinguisher toward him forcing him to fall to his knees.

"Then sit down and shut up." I calmly tell him before sitting on my trunk as I wait for the cops.

Damn, three niggas at me in one day! I must've really pissed somebody off. It's only one person I can think of who would come at me like this, but this wasn't really Emilio's style. I stand by while the cops work the scene. They had already questioned me and sent Highway Man on his way. I couldn't do anything but sit here and think. Most people would be in shock going through a day like this, but for me I was in my comfort zone.

***

"The notorious Vegas Wolfchild! I see somebody is on yo ass ta'day!" Hearing and seeing Detective Rooney snapped me back to the now. Rooney's one of the only detectives that I like, so him calling me by my whole name didn't piss me off that much, it's usually how he addresses me.

"Yeah, but I'm always a step or two ahead so that's why he on my ass and why this one's dead." Times like this I love to rub it in the cops' faces that it's more than likely I'll be getting away with another murder.

"What about that shit down from your office, this connected?"

"Like I said then, I'm saying now. I don't know what's going on." I understand why they wouldn't believe me, but I still don't like being asked the same question twice.

Detective Rooney was giving me a look as if he wasn't believing a word from my mouth.

"Well the Captain wants us to bring in B-."

"WHO SMOKEY!" I ask cutting him off. Rooney starts chuckling.

"Haven't heard nobody call him that since you left, but yeah him. But like I was saying we both know you not going in no squad car, so he's giving you 45 minutes to be at the station."

Damn I really just wanted to go home, shower, rest, and think. Shit, I haven't had the time to enjoy the feeling of finally fucking Ebony.

"Okay man, I gotta get my rental from Rev's across the bridge and I guess I'll go holla at Smokey." Sounding irritated and tired, but I knew for real things couldn't go more smoothly than it had been.

Years ago back when I was still on the force and undercover officer Steve Bale a.k.a. 'Smokey' was a beat cop. He fit the title he always looked beat like this shit on the streets was breaking him. He wasn't out of shape or nothing like that just 15-year vet wore out. Because he looked like a slim Smokey the Bear most people thought that was the reason I called him Smokey. Truth is while I was undercover I came across the fact that Officer Bale was a crack head. On a couple of occasions I served him myself. I guess he was thinking since he bought his crack on the Eastside no one would find out. We both were surprised when I came in from undercover and our paths crossed. I never let him know I was surprised. I always played it off like I had known he was a cop. Every time we meet, which is rarely, I remind him in secret of his crack smoking days. That's exactly what I'm doing now in his office as I sit across from him.

"Vegas, this is not your home, take your feet off my desk… Would you stop bringing up the fact that I was once a smoker." I can't stop myself from laughing because he sounded just like Smokey the Bear too. You are just waiting for him to say, "And only you can prevent forest fires!"

I respect his wishes and remove my feet.

"Thank you! Now tell me what's going on. Two bodies in less than 12 hours… Damn! Vegas, that's crazy."

"Shit, I don't know what to tell you, both attacks were surprises to me!" I tell him before taking a pen from his desk and I begin twirling it staring at the Captain.

"Look Vegas, I know you's a baaaad chick and everything, but you was once a cop so to me you'll always be a cop…" Smokey stops as if to find the right words. "If you really don't know why these people are coming after you maybe I can get you some protection. Lock you up a couple days or just put the word out that you are. I guess I kind of owe you so to a point I'll help you."

"How nice of you, Smokey. Thanks but I got my protection here." I tell him while patting my two babies.

He stares at me for a minute too long if you ask me and now that I know he feels like he owes me that's a card I would rather pull later.

"Well we didn't get anything from the two dead bodies." He was still staring at me like he expected me to say something. "Here, this was in their pockets."

"Okay Vegas, but know these attempts don't give you a reason to kill somebody. So if you use those it better be in self defense." The Captain paused with a smile letting me fill in the blanks.

Almost being killed and having the Captain threaten me put me in a certain mood as I fly down the lodge banging 2Pac… Man this shit crazy! I mean for sure I done some shit since I been back in the City, but nothing to bring this type of heat. Plus I haven't fucked with anybody who had it in them to come at me. For instance getting Jssiah out of that 60 ball and those bricks. For sure that's worth being killed, but he's not stupid enough to come at me even if he thought I'll never find out! Okay, what about the Dexter Boys? I did get three of them shot but the Dexter Boys or Jssiah didn't know I was playing both sides. It was something else about the way they came at me that had me dismissing the Dexter Boys and Jssiah as the people behind the attacks.

Hearing my phone ring took my attention from one problem to another because I see that it's Marcus who's calling. I'm no where in the mood to play with this nigga.

"What up doh?"

"You, I heard about the shit at yo spot, calling to make sure you alive." He chuckles… "What up wit that one thing?"

"You send the rest of that bread?"

"Vegas, come on… 30 too much. Let me send you 3 mo and let's leave it at that." This nigga don't know I'm already on the verge of fucking him over.

"You know what… I'm about to pull up on you!"

Pulling up to Marcus's spot, and despite the few cars in the driveway and in the front yard, his shit looked abandoned. There was no front door and no lights were on throughout the whole house. Shit didn't look inviting at all. That was the point I guess. Hopping out of my rental I walk up the driveway knowing that going through the front door was death around this time. By the time I was past the third car I was starting to hear voices and music. A side door opened up and still no light is coming from the house nor could I see anybody just the red beam aimed at me. This nigga Marcus thinks he the bad guy in a movie or something with this shit. Maybe if I didn't know him I'd be spooked I think as I walk into the dark entrance. Don't get me wrong, if somebody did just happen to show up uninvited Marcus was for sure feeding him to the dogs. It's just that I'm not the one to fuck with, Marcus is Trick's old owner and I'm still waiting for a reason to smoke his boots!

Just because the house looked fucked from the outside didn't mean it really was and since I had been here before I knew that. But Marcus built the basement for one reason only, and the music and the people here wasn't the evidence of a party. The loud weed smell couldn't hide the smell coming from the animals that fought, lost blood, and some lost their lives down here. How many so far this night I'll never know, but the crowd was super hype for the next fight and I heard big money being bet. I stop paying attention to the bets and the crowd and started to look for Marcus.

I see him standing in the middle of the ring. He was athletically built, about 6'1", light-skinned nigga with dreads. One of them niggas who think he can talk his way outta Hell but if he fuck wit me ta'night he gonna find out he can talk his way into Hell too! That's just how I'm feeling ta'night... Yeah because if I'm not mistaken I think that's a dog's ear that lay by his feet! I know I'm around here shooting and killing niggas, but this life was chosen by us. These dogs didn't choose shit, they was just born dogs, it pisses me off the way these niggas treat animals. I'm just going to fall back because I'll fuck around kill somebody. Marcus seen me so he knows I'm here.

Marcus had a few bad bitches in here and I seen a few take niggas upstairs. I was talking to one of these freaks when Marcus finally made his way to where I was.

"Vegas, what up doh!" Marcus yells over the music throwing up both his hands and coming in for a handshake. "Here go yo bread."

"Whoa!" I push his hand back. "Send that shit over the wire. Plus that look 15 bands light!"

"I thought over the phone we…" I cut him off raising my hands as I look around making sure we weren't being overheard before I say what I'm about to say.

"Just stop man, listen, if I'm not mistaken you want this info so you can not 'Talk'," I stare at him to make sure we had an understanding. "So 30 thou sounds cheap for a cop life." I say looking and feeling tired and bored.

"That's crazy!" Marcus says smiling. "Talk is all I want to do Vegas… So take this three and that'll be 18 an give me the info."

"A nigga paying 18 for a conversation, NOW THAT SOUNDS CRAZY!" I say hoping he can hear the irritation in my voice and how stupid he sounds.

"Yeah, that do sound crazy, but I got it!" He says still smiling… I put my head down and shake it. Irritated now to the max by him and the cheering from the crowd watching the dogs fight. But I make sure I keep my emotions in check.

"Marcus, you want me to blow yo fuckin' brains out!" He look around and I don't know if it's to make sure I wasn't heard or to make a point.

"You think you'll feel better in Hell knowing that after I killed you yo boys killed me? Because I don't think you will… Now no matter what you not getting the 15 bands back. This case is closed, either you send me the rest of my money and get the information you're asking for or I let the cop know you're asking around for his personal info." I say this then I turn around and leave while the crowd goes bananas for whatever reason.

CHAPTER 6

Not really wanting to drive to my loft last night I called Tots to make sure she wasn't having nobody over. I don't play that fucking while I'm in the house shit! But she wasn't so I slept in her spare room.

Waking up refreshed and energized I promised to start on one if not both of my new cases today. I have to admit with muthafuckas already at my head coming at Marcus like that last night probably wasn't smart but fuck it. I hop out the shower and check my latest wounds. My stitches were still good, I'll just have to change the bandages…

Dressed in something similar to what I had on yesterday I step into the hallway to the smell of bacon and see Tot's flat ass in a cute matching silk pajama short set. One thing for sure, friend or not, a fine-ass bitch like Tots can't stand in front of me dressed like that and expect me not to admire her. Flat ass and all she was cold and because I seen her naked I knew her body was evenly toned, so sitting at her small table in the kitchen I admired her body for a second…

"What's this, the Tot's special bacon and toast?" I say with a couple strips of bacon in hand. I mean she can't scramble eggs! Tots laughs still with her back to me turning off the stove.

"Nigga bitch you know I can't cook!" She says chuckling.

"What you talking about? This bacon good as hell!" We both chuckle a little.

"So what's up? What you doing that you got niggas bussing at you?"

"Man, I don't know yet! Shit just coming out the blue."

Once again I fall back into deep thought racking my brain and still coming up empty. The cops probably thought I was holding something back, but Tots knew if I had a real problem or knew why niggas was on my ass she'll be the first person I'll come to, we been in too much shit already.

"Have you thought maybe it's... Emilio?" Tots asks barely looking up from her plate. I can understand why she'd ask it like that. Nobody really knew how I felt about talking about Emilio since I haven't talked about him or my kidnapping since I returned, but really Emilio's just a person I don't think about often.

"Naw, this ain't his style. I don't think he'll send somebody to kill me. He'll want to do that himself."

I look at Tots with a smile on my face because the thought of Emilio coming after me is something I'll welcome.

"Nigga, you crazy if I was you he'd be that last muthafucka that'll bring a smile to my face." Tots said as if she was reading my mind. Getting up Tots leaves the kitchen and returns with a comb and stands behind my chair.

"Let me put this back in a braid for you. You want me to cut this other side for you too?" Tots says sounding serious.

"Bitch stop playing!"

Tots laugh. "What? It's only a bald head... Vegas, I gotta tell you something... I'm pregnant."

"...WHAT?!" It took me a minute for it to register.

Tots tug on my head and resumes gathering my hair.

"Yeah bitch, I don't know how. Me and Church use protection. Muthafucka must of busted and he didn't tell me." Tots said sounding shocked.

"So it's Clay's?"

"Yeah bitch! He the only nigga I'm fuckin' but he don't know that. I told him I had a nigga. So he thinks we both cheating." Tots chuckles as she shakes her head. I didn't know what to say or think. Like we be in a lot of shit and for real Tots is worried about Emilio coming after me she gotta know or at least think that he knew that her and Mo was a part of the robbery.

"You keeping the baby?"

"Hell yeah! I don't know… What you think?" Tots was sounding unsure and I was glad she wasn't looking at me because I had no answers. Shit, she could keep the baby. It's not like she'll be raising him on her own.

"Yeah, fuck it! Keep the little homie. Lord knows I'm not having no kids… We for sure can raise a child you, Moose and me." I say and I don't know why but I was liking the idea.

"What about Church?" Tots sounded unsure still. I don't know why, all the shit we done. Fuck! Keeping this from Clay should be the easiest thing to do.

"Hoe, what about him? Not only is he married but he the Mayor too! And didn't you just say he think you got a nigga? So let 'em keep thinking that… Plus Cherish paying me to find out who he's cheating with, so he's…"

"What! Whoa bitch back up. She got you doing what?" Tots stops braiding my hair and goes and sits across from me. Shit, I was going to have to tell her anyways and on some real shit she need to stop fuckin' him if she plan to have this kid.

"Tots, stop playing wit me and finish my hair." I try to sound serious but Tots wasn't buying it. She folded her arms and stares at me…

So I tell Tots how Cherish called me and I tell her about our meeting. I leave out any and everything to do with Ebony. Nobody knew about my high school crush on her.

"Since I knew it was you he was fuckin' I wasn't really gonna do nothing. Just get some money outta her and act like he wasn't cheating." Tots put her head down.

"I can't believe this shit... Cherish?" Tots whisper sounding confused. I'm sure she thought her and the Mayor were slick with they shit. Probably the same way Ebony thought she was. I wouldn't be surprised at all if Cherish was hip to her too.

"Why not Ebony?" I look at her confused. "Why is it Cherish and not Ebony who's paying you?" That's a good question. One that needed an answer to.

"Shit, I don't know, but fuck it. I'm on the case so you cool. Now get back to my hair."

But now that I think about it I really need to know why Ebony's not concerned about her husband cheating. Or maybe she is and she been complaining to Mom and Cherish decided to take things into her own hands. Maybe that's what Ebony was doing yesterday, fuckin' me... Damn, I wonder when the next time she going to let me...

"Nah! You know what? You should really do yo P.I. shit, Vegas." Tots interrupts my thoughts. Now she got me wondering what's up her sleeve.

"Well, you know if I was planning to really do work I would've got more out her ass!"

"What's today, Wednesday? I'm back on his detail tomorrow and I'll break it off with him then. I'm sure he'll be fucking another soon. Shit he probably is now!"

"Hoe, you sound like you missing that shit already! I bet you fuckin' him tomorrow!"

"Nigga bitch hell yeah!" Tots says laughing.

Usually when I have a case like these I hire my little brother Gage. He's a nerdy-looking photographer who's good at surveillance like that with a camera and other electronics. Plus he got that "don't mind me I'm a bitch nigga" look. So people say and do shit around him without thinking. I call and put him on the Mayor's line. I wouldn't be surprised if I get pictures of the Mayor in the hotel room. I won't mind seeing Tots in action. With

Cherish, and now Tots, I was able to get the Mayor's itinerary for the next week. This case shouldn't last any longer... For the money it won't end no sooner!

With that in the bag I turn my mind to Flex, really feeling like he's somebody I should do a background check on. Especially if he gonna be in my City, plus he claim to be from here. Now that I think about it... Flex could be the nigga gunning for me. But why? He want yo spot Vee... Hell Nah! Can't another muthafucka do what I do... Okay, Okay. Then maybe she just want you out her way. My bad... HIS way. (Chuckling) I'm fucked up talking to myself like this! Well that's stupid because it's a lot of muthafuckas in his way and I'm not one of them.

Look around, there's so many niggas and bitches getting money in the City and yes, I got something on some of them but not all, and I'm not stopping them from getting money. It's just best to work with me than against me if our paths should cross... Thinking about this got me thinking about Marcus's bitch ass. He might not know it but there's a greater chance that I'll kill him than turn him over to a crooked cop. I checked my account and I see the money hit. Marcus isn't as stupid as I thought or as much as I wished he was. But I can see him making me kill him one of these times.

"Joyce, what up?" I have to be careful when fuckin' with niggas like Marcus so that's why I was talking to Joyce now.

"Why haven't you called your father? You know he's worried about you!" Joyce snaps on me.

"I thought that was what you was for, to stop him from worrying." I start chuckling.

"Funny... Make sure you call him. Now what you want? I thought kicking me out the office was like you sending me on vacation or something!"

"Uuuuum NO! I need you to contact Spokes. Tell'em ta go by the kennel and grab a few mutts from Moose, she knows what's up." After that shit last night I don't know. I can see that nigga Marcus getting caught and turning rat. Gotta cover all bases thirty thou for a few mutts sounds crazy. Marcus doesn't know. But he done bought a hundred mutts this past week. These will just be the first he receives. Even though I wasn't paying too much attention to Joyce that didn't stop her from lecturing me on my behavior toward Rev. Of course she was right, but shit he'll understand.

Being in this rental and not in my bulletproof Charger I was feeling kind of naked. Even though I was probably a little more safe moving around in this because it was a small chance anybody knows about this rental. It's nothing like being bulletproof. This morning I sent a picture of Katrina A.K.A. Kitty around to a couple busto's who move like her. So if she shows up I'll know, but I'm cruising down Michigan Ave just like I did on Woodward. I really don't expect to see her as I scan the strip.

She's a little too young and bad still to be out here, but I gotta cover all the bases and that's one of the reasons I'm going to hit up the Eastside. Holla at Slick plus I just wanna fuck wit him and get a good laugh, it's been a while. Remembering the last time I had a run in with Slick it was a classic moment. Slick is an Eastside pimp. White out of town runaways is his specialty. But if Kitty is halfway as open as her pictures suggest and if her and Slick's paths cross I'm sure Slick will use her up quickly. Turning off Shane and heading up Mack I whip into Slick's driveway to his four-family flat. You used to be able to find these flats all over the City, but not so much nowadays.

Slick is surrounded by three white girls no older than 23 and I was stretching that. It was more like they were 19 and younger. The scene I was looking up at was crazy. This super slim black-ass nigga being pampered by three of the palest white bitches I ever seen! He was taking it a step farther by having them dressed in all white and he himself in all black, silly nigga here! Hopping out my rental I couldn't help but smile. Slick had one bitch brushing his waves, one filing his nails, and the other bitch was holding a pistol. Why? I don't know...

First off I would've been stomped Slick's little ass out so putting a gun in my hand was out of the question. So yeah, I found this scene funny as hell.

"You must treat that bitch real good for her not to shoot you." I say to Slick as I approach the steps.

"What! That's ah negative… Picture Slick treating a how any other way than the way a how should be treated." Slick had this smooth way of talking. This why I fuck with Slick. He really thinks he the slickest pimp ever.

"You got it backwards, Vegas… That hoe must be treating me good, for me not to have her shoot herself… Ain't that right Pussy?"

"That's what you telling me Slick." The white girl says with the gun sounding like a horny slave. I chuckle as I lean on the steps.

"Damn, Slick, I know it's been a minute since we chopped it up but you looking old up there. I see a couple great whites swimming up there." Pointing out the grays but Slick couldn't be no more than 41-42 years old.

"Yeah grays come with waking up everyday. Along with my 3 Snow Whites kissing my lips, dick, and toes!"

The mannerism of Slick always have me caught up. The way he move and talk. How his hoe's not look at him and laugh is the question.

"Alright Slick! Fuckin' wit you I'll be here all day, but I need some info… no bullshit." I say making sure he understands it wasn't no ratting shit going on. One more thing I respect about Slick. From experience I know he's solid. Slick sends his hoes in the house.

"Can't let a hoe hear nothing but do this, do that. And Vegas don't let a hoe see nothing if it ain't pointing… I'm talking my dick or my finger!"

"Come on Slick!" I say laughing… "On some real shit you pick up something new?"

"Nah, these new hoes out here hardheaded. I tell a hoe I want her here Monday at 6:00pm with 5 grand… She think it's alright if she's here Tuesday at 6 with 8 grand!" Slick look up to the sky like he asking for help!

"Got a bitch in there now surprised that my red bottoms fit perfectly in her ass!"

Man I really didn't want to encourage Slick but I can't help it, the nigga is a nut!

"Damn Slick she brought you back three extra grand for…" Slick cut me off!

"See, see! That's where muthafuckas go wrong! Them 12 bitches in there," Slick says pointing toward his house. "They don't go get that chicken cause they want to! Nooooo! Vegas, it's cause Slick tell them to! That's a negative. Picture one of Slick's hoes doing what she want, huh? You better believe Slick wanted it first."

I haven't stopped laughing since I stepped out of my rental. But I had to stop Slick knowing from past experiences that he is long-winded. I guess he be needing a different audience from his hoes. I put up both hands asking him to calm down!

"Slick, I want you to look at this pic and if you seen her put me in the loop and if you see her hit my hip." I pull out my phone and show Slick Kitty's Instagram. Why I do that? As if the phone was on fire Slick quickly tosses the phone back to me. Damn this nigga was extra! Slick pushed a door bell he keeps on his lap. Instantly white girls start filing out the door like doves. Blondes, brunettes, redheads, I even see one with dreads, and they were all sizes. I was seriously shocked at the 11 beauties he had in his stable. I seen one I might come back and fuck wit.

"Vegas, look at my stable!" This is the closest I ever seen Slick serious, I mean sound serious, that one line.

"You see any black hoes? NO! Check it Vegas… Only time my hoe ain't white is when you turn off the light… Train or flight! Bus or bike! If you young and white come find Slick and better yo life!"

After kissing all 11 of his hoes he points them back into the house like dogs. Still chuckling, but I no longer had the patience to go through another one of Slick's spills.

"Alright Slick I'm gone man! I'll catch up wit you later, thanks." I scream as I hop back in the rental. I knew it was a long shot wit Slick but it was worth the laugh and the tension in my body has eased. Being back on the Eastside had me wanting to stop by a couple of my other connects. Now that I think about it I should've brought them bricks I got off Jssiah and got them shift and broke down. I was up to doing anything to stop me from thinking about the attempts on my life. Something going to drop in my lap, you don't come at me in my City and none of my people know nothing about it.

Later that evening I finally made my way to the Holy Water. Stepping into the bar like most times, I stop after a few steps and look around as my eyes get used to the dim room. Rev love Detroit music so more times than not Anita Baker is playing through the bar. I don't know if it's just a coincidence or a sign that the song 'I Apologize' is on. I hum along looking for Rev, seeing him I walk toward him across the bar. Knowing I been acting too much like a bastard and Joyce along with Anita Baker had me feeling some type of way.

"Pops!" I yell from a few feet away to get his attention from the news he was watching. Seeing the smile on his face made me feel like a teenager again as I give him a long hug.

Never have I not felt loved by my father growing up. My mother died when I was 6 years old. When I was 14 I learned about the role my Pops played in her and her twin brother's death, Moose's father. My mother and her brother were stick up kids. My father would sell drugs then have them rob the dudes he just sold the drugs to, then he would break the drugs down and resell it back to them cheaper as if he felt sorry for them. Like most times something goes wrong, now my moms and Moose's pops are dead. At 14 when I learned this from him it fucked me up, that's when I started depending on myself more. Those feelings most likely played a major role in my decision to be a cop. Which I am far from… I'm more likely to get somebody killed than locked up. Me seeing that as a positive may cause for some looking into by a professional but fuck it. No matter what my pops supported me and always gave me space to grow with little input. Times like this he probably regrets that.

"You not tripping that I didn't call you ASAP?" I ask Rev as he steps behind the bar to grab two shot glasses and a bottle.

"Shit Vegas, I know how you are, plus if you wasn't fine what the fuck! I wasn't gonna be able to stop what was done already." Like any father I guess Rev felt some type of way about not being able to keep me from harm.

"Nah, I wasn't tripping. I'm both mad and happy that you're so fucking tough, Vegas. I know you blame me for your OG and Uncle's deaths, but I couldn't control her young ass no more than I can you."

My mother was 23 when she was killed she would've been 44 this year.

"But that's what I love about both of you. Like I told you before, this is your life and everything that happens in it you cause some way or another. Like I miss Ruby and mourned her death, the fact is life goes on. If something happens to you Vegas… (putting his head down shaking it)… Something happens to you Vegas it will crush me and I'll mourn longer… But life goes on for the living. So remember shoot first and we'll deal wit the other shit later!" Rev says as he and I toast to another day and down our shots.

CHAPTER 7

Sitting in my office at Rev's I contact all my workers, I still couldn't find Cherry. One of my girls I usually have work the floor. I was telling my workers that the Backroom is closed and that I'll cash app them two bans each, the money stops all the questions. Closing the spot down was a must. It wasn't a secret that Rev was my pops and he for sure was in danger too, but what could I really do to stop that? Sitting here cleaning my guns with these thoughts, after that father and daughter moment I really need to find out who's on my line quick.

Hearing my bell ring tells me Rev is bringing somebody back here that I wasn't expecting or somebody I usually wouldn't see here. Loading my one cleaned pistol I leave the other one in pieces. Even though I knew Rev wouldn't lead anyone back here strapped. Still I sit on my desk, pistol gripped loosely in my hand dangling between my legs.

I was surprised as ever to see Short Fuse walk through my door. He was one of if not the most respected shooters in the Dee, from the Westside. At a time like this any other shooter would've been shot on sight, but I give Rev a nod letting him know it's cool.

"Shooter man! What up doh!?" I say as we embrace like old friends, which we were, unknown to most. Standing 5'9" Short Fuse was a dark skin nigga with a nappy afro. If you was stupid enough to judge him by his slim frame your judgement would change once you looked into his eyes. There is no mistaking what you see in them. Short Fuse was for no games with a pistol in his hands and the name Short Fuse fit him well. What some would let go as nothing would set him off, you never knew what he took as disrespect. His services weren't cheap and what is also unknown to all who hired him was that once he accepted a hit from you he'll be watching your family for the next year.

"You know. The same ol' same." Short Fuse says in his nonchalant way as he takes a sip from his flask. "I heard about them niggas on yo line and that's why I'm here. I got some info for you." I holster my pistol and start pacing.

"It's this site on the dark web. I'm not telling you the name so don't ask. Just know it's a site for shooters."

"How did you find the site?" Him not telling me the name of the site, I didn't take as disrespect. Knowing him he just saw it as none of my business.

"Like I told you... it's for shooters. You gotta be invited in and it still gonna cost you 10 racks to get to the questionnaire part if you interested. But if you really like that then 10 rack ain't nothing because you for sure going to triple that at least wit no problem." Short Fuse tells me with a smile looking up at me as he begin to play with Tricks. "But the thing is, Vegas, once you on this site you get the chance to make big money. Every time you log in it's no less than 50 hits listed. All over, not just the City!" He pauses after saying that and I stop and look at him.

"Yeah! A nigga in Detroit can easily take a hit in Mississippi."

"Sooo, what? It's a hit on me?" I ask looking a little confused. I mean I'm a problem but that's a lot of work to get to me.

"Yeah, it's a hun bun on you head Vegas."

"Sheesh! A hundred thou! Nigga you smiling, this shit ain't cute!" I snap, "Is there anything specific or they just want me dead?"

"It's a hundred to grab you and contact a number. You only get that once the shooter post you on the site. I'm sure there are other instructions after that. It drops all the way to 25k just to pop you."

"Mmmm." Okay that makes sense and that's why the first nigga didn't just open up on me once he saw me. I'm thinking this as I pace around my office.

"All the shooters in the City that's on the site we came together and said trying you wasn't worth it. Niggas know you lethal for real. Plus on the low I was gonna double back and knock off whoever thought they wanted to try you. But I guess Shawn thought differently. I hear he was found in ashes in you alley." Short Fuse smirks.

"Yeah, I ain't fuckin' around. A hundred on my head is disrespect!" I say smiling.

"Yeah, you see that a lot but you the first hunnit thou in the City tho."

I was feeling a little better knowing where the heat is coming from but still I gotta find out who think they can have my head.

"It's really no need for me to ask you to put yo reputation on the line and help me set the muthafucka up who's after me, huh?"

"Vegas, I can't do that, but you know if you need me I'm around." I can hear his disappointment. After saying that Short Fuse stands up.

"Respect, respect. I feel you. Thanks for putting me in the loop. I owe you one."

Waking up to my phone buzzing like crazy alerting me that I was getting a video message. Not wanting to stay at Tots again or drive to my loft I crashed in the office on my leather couch last night. Snatching up my phone I open the video message… If I was still sleepy I wasn't no more at the vision of Ebony in the shower slowly soaping her soft chocolate skin. This bitch was sexy and this video was already turning me the fuck on.

Taking the shower head Ebony turns toward the camera as she let the water slowly rinse the soap away. Clearing the view to her shiny skin and her long nipples that she takes her time pinching. Oh my god her skin was beautiful. Biting my lower lip as I watch her hands roam her body massaging her titties and pulling on her nipples…

"Damn!" I whisper as I untie my joggers. I slide my hands in my panties and they were already soaking just from looking at Ebony's naked body. Damn my nipples were begging to be touched, so I start rubbing them through my shirt and bra.

Ebony causes me to suck in a breath when she bent over. Seeing her puffy pussy hang there brought back memories from the other day when I had my face buried in there. Ebony reached between her legs and spread her pussy lips.

"Vegas, you remember this pretty pussy?" Do I! I can taste it now, I think as I see her juices overflowing her box.

"I came early thinking of you eating this." Ebony continues to tease me as she traced her pussy hole.

Turning to face the camera Ebony lifts her leg on the edge of the tub. She was killing me stuffing two fingers in her box. Taking them out Ebony makes sure she shows them to the camera and lets me see the juices covering her fingers. I could hear her moaning as she cleaned her honey from her fingers looking into the camera.

"FUCK!" Quickly removing my clothes I begin feeling my juices sliding between my ass crack as I sit back on the couch. Opening my legs wide as I toss one leg on the back of the couch. I slide my hands all over my trembling body. I was on fire! Dragging a finger against my wet slit, "Ohhhh!" I was so wet and ready to cum.

Ebony took the shower nozzle and adjusted the shower speed. I could clearly see Ebony's chest moving, we were both breathing fast. All women done had they turn with the shower head so I knew the amazing feeling Ebony was anticipating.

"Cum with me, Vegas." She moaned as she sit on the tub and opened her legs placing her feet on the wall.

"God yes!" I softly say as I start rubbing my clit slowly at first as Ebony separated her pussy lips wider and wider, exposing her sweet pussy to me and the shower head.

I softly repeat, "Oh my God. God, oh yes!" When I start rubbing my clit faster before licking and nibbling on my small nipples. "That's it, that's it, ohhhh yessss!" I was moaning loudly now. Rubbing my clit I was on the brink of a morning nut...

Just as I was cumming Brittany came into my office, not stopping I close my eyes and expose more of my pussy to her.

"I thought I heard you in here moaning," she says in a sexy voice. I continue to cum and moan as I rub my pussy. Opening my eyes, with Brittany coming in I was getting extra horny. Brittany locked the door and began walking toward me.

"I been wanting to taste you since I met you, Vegas!" I had to put the phone down to play with my nipples before Brittany walked in, but you could hear Ebony moaning before the message ended. Brittany removed my hand from my throbbing clit and replaced them with her lips...

High yellow with light brown eyes Brittany is a super petite 22-year-old. Now laying naked with me on my couch under a blanket. What's better than starting your day with two nuts and the taste of some good pussy!

"Vegas, I know you been through some shit, but all these scars are crazy." Brittany says as she traces my scars and lightly kiss them making sure to stay away from my wounds that were still stitched. I keep my mouth shut as I think about how to deal with this. Not that I'm against fuckin' somebody that works for me, and I liked Brittany, but this was a crazy surprise.

"Ummmm, Vegas, you don't know how wet my pussy got hearing you moaning in here like that. Just thinking about it I'm getting wet again!" The way she sounded so horny I had to take my hand and see for myself.

"Damn!" I whisper... Fuck it. I play with her pussy for a bit before going down on her making her cum again all over my face and fingers...

"So why you come in today? I told you to take the week off." I whisper in her ear before sucking the rest of the cum off my fingers and getting up off the couch and picking up my clothes.

"Damn! Why you stop?" Brittany whines, pouting with those pretty-ass lips. Pulling the blanket back showing me her shaved pussy. Damn, seeing that muthafucka I was tempted.

"Don't worry, that thang too tasty and too good to only have once." I say this but looking at her and knowing her I knew I was going to have to be more firm with her to get my point across. "Brittany, you know the reason I gave you the week off. Muthafuckas tryin to kill me, so you can't be here! I'm glad you came through and put those pretty muthafuckas to work, but you need to get yo ass up and dressed!" Brittany looked like she was getting the picture because her look went from sexy to understanding.

"Vegas, I understand and now that you know I fuck around just get at me sometime." Brittany gets up and picks her panties up off the floor. Damn… I had to turn around and step into my little restroom. Having nothing but a toilet and a sink I couldn't call it a bathroom.

Face washed and breath smelling fresh I come back into my office and Brittany's pretty ass is still here. So I knew whatever she was here to tell me had to be important to her.

"What's up? Put me in the loop."

"Well, I came to tell you Cherry is missing." Not knowing what type of response she was expecting all I could do was look at her. In no type of way did I feel Cherry was my responsibility.

"Don't you care that she's missing?" Brittany snaps!

"I care that she didn't tell me she was leaving, that way I could've hired somebody else!" I tell her as I sit behind my desk.

"She was scared to tell you she was leaving. I tried to stop her but she been on her Christian shit!"

"The fuck you talking about?" 8:00am was too fucking early for this. I was wondering why Brittany would think I would give a fuck. Her pussy was good, but unless she had some money I wasn't going to look for Cherry… That bitch was a whole woman!

"Well, a couple weeks ago, maybe longer I don't know when she really started, but Cherry been talking about forgiving people and shit. Said she been in contact with Quan."

"WHO! Fat Cat Quan?" I ask very shocked expecting her to say no.

"Yeah, Fat Cat Quan. I told her she was tripping."

"Hell yeah that bitch tripping!" I was pissed and right now I'm feeling like whatever happens to her is really not my concern.

Around five years ago Quan owned a magazine called 'Fat Cat Purr!' Brittany and Cherry worked for him as models. Cherry was completely different from Brittany in looks. Cherry was a chocolate Amazon of a woman; Serena Williams like but better looking by far. That's the only way to describe her. That or just a bad bitch! I'm talking tall, super thick, and sexy as fuck. Anyways, Quan invited them to a private party after a photo shoot. No more than nine people outside of the five models that were there. He drugged them, then him and a few of his friends raped then. I wouldn't have believed it without proof, but Moose was there and you know she was all on Brittany's line that night… (Which I'm going to make sure she knows I fucked. Get her back for buying that truck.) Moose left early, but not before getting Brittany's number. The next day Moose called trying to line something up and Brittany cried over the phone as she told Moose what happened when she left the party, which led to this…

On a very cold night dressed in all black I open the door to my U-Haul unit I had my guy Boots behind me. Boots it 6'6", 320 lbs, a solid but kinda fat nigga. I call him Boots because he known for kicking doors in since forever. At that time Boots was out of prison for about a year and he was back smoking and on his bullshit. So he was perfect for this job. Boots closed the door behind us and I turned on the light.

Quan's chubby ass was naked bending over a table, wrists cuffed to rings coming from the tabletop and his ankles cuffed to the table legs. Quan was looking up at me and I saw the fear and hatred in his eyes. I understood both since I had him in here like that for the past ten hours.

"Boots, take the tape from his mouth." I lay my pistol down on the table and pull out my phone.

"Vegas, what the fuck! For the last two months I been paying you," he says, crying. "Come on, don't do this!" Quan was referring to the six grand I been having him pay me since learning about his raping. That was cool until I learned he was back at it.

"Don't do what?" I ask as I slowly dial Moose's number.

"Come on I got two kids... don't do this Vegas!" Quan continued to beg.

I nod to Boots and he starts undressing in front of Quan, who is now openly crying real tears.

"Moose, they there?" I turn the phone around so they could see Quan's crying ass. Boots continues to undress.

"Can y'all see everything?" I ask as Boots starts to play with his dick.

"Vegas, this muthafucka might not get up!" Boots says in his deep voice.

Before I didn't know if Boots ever fucked a nigga... I pull out an ounce of crack and put it on the table. Funny what crack will make a smoker do. Boots started working his shit faster and talking to his dick. This big nigga's dick was huge! You could hear Brittany and Cherry say, "DAMN!" once Boot's shit was fully hard.

Quan seen it too as he started begging and shaking.

"Don't do this Vegas, I'm so sorry! Please, PLEASE!!!"

"Just like you took that pussy like a bitch nigga! Take that dick like a bitch nigga!" I spit at Quan and told Boots to go to work...

The scream that Quan let out was deafening and it only got worse with every pump. It was satisfying hearing the crying and screaming coming from Quan. Taking the phone and moving to the back I give them on the other end a view of the nasty shit that was going on. Shit and blood was all on Boots' dick and running down his legs. You could hear Cherry and Brittany crying on the other end along with Quan.

"You want me to buss in this bitch, Vegas?" Buss what! This nigga Boots was a sick nigga.

"Naw Boots, buss on his ass like he a bitch!" I move back so I can see Quan's face as Boots disrespects him.

"Now Quan, you got a chance to walk outta here alive." I tell him this as I empty the bullets out of my clip.

"Us three in here, plus the two bitches you raped and my cousin… She's a cop." I say this and look over to Quan making sure he understood the situation.

"Us six are the only ones who know what happened here ta'nite." I look over to Boots who's sitting in the corner smoking crack, still naked. I shake my head at this sick nigga…

I unlock Quan's wrists but not his ankles.

"Ahhhh! Ohhhh!" Quan lets out. I guess he was feeling sore, but it also had to feel good to stand, tears continued to run down his face.

"Like I was saying, you can leave out of here and live and ever be free. I'm going to give you a chance to get some pay back… This gun still has a bullet in the head. You can shoot me… or you can shoot the nigga that fucked you."

Boots was high but not that high I guess because he hear that and Boots quickly look up at me spaced out.

"Vegas, stop playing." Boots said before going back to his crack pipe.

If Boots knew how much he made me sick he would've known I wasn't playing when I handed my pistol to Quan who waited a minute. I guess he had to think. He raised the pistol and aimed it at Boots and pulled the trigger. Nothing happened. Quan pulled the trigger again and again yelling in frustration. Boots took long enough but finally he got up and rushed Quan tackling him on the table. Quan was no match for Boots with his legs still cuffed to the table legs. I was hearing bones crush as Boots beat Quan bloody…

"Boots!" I yell trying to get his attention and once he looked up I pull out my other pistol and quickly shoot Boots twice in the face.

Now after that this bitch in here telling me Cherry went to find this nigga to give and get forgiveness. What the fuck? After that I don't remember the last time I saw Quan.

"So did she find him?" I ask not hiding my irritation.

"She said she found somebody linked to him."

"Then that's where she at. Fuck it!" I get up and sling my holster over my back.

"Yeah, but why she haven't called or answered my calls?" Brittany asks and I can hear and see her concern for her friend's well-being, but it didn't move me. I still didn't know what she expected from me and I asked her that.

"Do your investigation thing!" she says with some flare.

"She was fucking Seven, you ask him if she contacted him?" Brittany looked surprised that I knew that. Wonder what she'll think if I told her I got tape of Cherry and Seven fuckin' in his truck.

"I didn't think you knew about them. But yes, I asked him, and he knew less than me and he seemed worried too. So you gonna find her?" Brittany crossed her arms and cocked her head and smiled at me.

So of course I agreed to help but really I had little to no intentions of putting that much energy into it. Like I said, I haven't heard or seen him in years. With money on my head and cases I'm working on already I doubt I'll have the time anyway to be looking for a stupid bitch, and I was tempted to say this to Brittany. But her tongue was down my throat and my phone was vibrating and then she was leaving before the thought left my mind.

CHAPTER 8

It was a video from one of my connects. Opening it I see a clear video of Kitty at an upscale strip club. This was a big shock because the scene didn't match her image; at least to me it didn't. As I continue to watch I notice it's one of my low-key spots, "Club Subtract." I put my phone away and head out the door with plans to stop by my loft, shower, and then head to Club Subtract.

Club Subtract was exactly that. Customers or dancers. While they subtracting clothes from their bodies you'll be subtracting money from your pocket, make no doubt about it. It's the only strip club in the City where money isn't thrown or seen. If you're one of them niggas who like to flash his money, this club is not for you.

Before actually entering the club you give your cash to a cashier and it's charged to a card. All tables have a machine attached to it and all dancers come with a number. There's no roll over or money back, cards deactivate upon leaving the club. Making sure that all money on the card is spent on dancers or drinks.

ALL GOOD A WEEK AGO

They were doing everything to keep B.S. from the club stamping its reputation as an upscale strip club. It's where I come to do a lot of business. They have a lot of back rooms for whatever type of business you're into.

I was coming from one of those rooms now after talking to a security guard, looking at footage of Kitty's couple hours at the club. The girl in the video handled herself nothing like who her Instagram would have you believe. Kitty was very chill and she kept looking back or at her watch, never really interested in the dancers. I was thinking of coming back later tonight and find out if and who she left with. With thoughts of Kitty and wondering of ways I could contact her I missed Flex's ugly ass ducked off in the corner. I would've continued to walk past him if he never called me...

A surprise for sure and a reminder that I gotta get that glass to my guy at the police station. Kitty here last night and Flex here now? Shit just didn't seem to add up. I may be paranoid, but Club Subtract wasn't the place you'll see Kitty's and Flex's at.

"Fuck you doing here?" I ask as I approach Flex's table not hiding my dislike for him.

Flex seemed not to take offense to my tone and answered my question.

"Just like you, I seen Katrina post on social media last night and she was here."

Damn, I haven't even been checking her shit. What the fuck, I never really had any real intentions of taking this case and I was really hoping he gave me reason to shoot him in the future.

"Do this seem like the type of strip club she'll be at?"

"Naw, not at all. This spot too laid back and bitches in here ain't even thick! I don't see why you be coming here." Flex says as he looks around. It was just about noon, the club at the time had about six business-looking men and two dancers were occupying their attention. But not mine. I heard what Flex just said, but I'll keep the slip to myself it was just more reason for me to get that glass to my guy ASAP. Something just wasn't right about this nigga, other than him having perfect titties and dressed in heels... Fuck Kitty! Who is this nigga! That's what I need to be finding out!

"Damn Mayor Church, you haven't given me my weekly dose." A woman says in a sex-deprived voice.

"Please tell me you had panties on during the meeting?" The Mayor says, but I didn't have to see him because the excitement in his voice said he wanted to hear otherwise.

"I make sure I don't wear any when I am around you... That way you can quickly get to this... Umm see how it's dripping on the seat?"

"Uh-huh!" You hear hard breathing and the sound of a belt unbuckling.

"Pull it out... Oh come on, Clay!" The woman begs in a sexy way.

You hear sucking sounds and moaning as the Mayor encourage the woman on. Obviously enjoying some good head and more.

Gage was liking every bit of what he was hearing. We were at my Coney Island and Gage was looking like the nerd he was. All bones and glasses. I had to force him to finish his Coney dog and fries. He was obviously excited still, I can only imagine how many times he listened to this tape and jerked off. Gage says he got to the Mayor's business meeting as the Mayor was leaving and he never got the chance to see the woman in the car. The driver left the car and went to a deli across the street once the Mayor got it. I asked him how he got the audio but he never tells me these things so I wasn't expecting him to this time either. But like always I was impressed by his work.

"So do you recognize the woman's voice on the tape?" Gage asks with his mouth full.

Hell yeah I recognize the voice and that was making this case very interesting, but leaving me with more questions than answers.

I wasn't about to tell Gage that I knew the woman that was sucking and fucking the Mayor in the car was the Mayor's Mother-In-Law not only that, she was the woman that hired me!

ALL GOOD A WEEK AGO

"Nope! But that's what we was hired to find out so stay on his line and this time Gage... don't bust a nut in your super mans and keep following the fucking car!"

Gage started choking when I got to super mans and was still choking when I got up and left.

School was out so I wasn't surprised to see kids running around when I slowly turned on to Ridgewood. It just means I'll have to be more alert. Like having a ticket on yo head wasn't enough!

Scar had been at the Kennel so I didn't have his help and the garage trick was used up, plus not being in my Bat-Mobile was also against me. So yeah, I was more cautious than ever as I crept past my crib. Nothing was out of place so I enter the alley to get to my garage and get the glass out of my trunk.

Exiting with glass in hand a step and a half clear of the garage and shots rung out! They were coming from my right and they were low. Leg shots! Lucky the rental was there and took the first shots in the fender and tires. I drop down and draw my two pistols as I ran to the rear of the car. Shit was feeling like déjà vu! Thank God this was a shooter looking to get the hundred thou!

The alley was split by an island of grass and trees and the shooter was coming from the other side of the island. Peeking around the car I seen him standing there aiming two pistols of his own.

"Little nigga you just drawing attention, polic-."

The shooter let off another series of shots drowning out my words. I let off a couple blind shots and then peeked around to see how the shooter moved.

Confident in his bulletproof vest the nigga didn't move at all before lighting the rental up. A few of his shots seemed like they were close to hitting me, another reason why I needed to be back in my Charger! I can't stay like this, plus I was hearing sirens in the distance. This area wasn't used to this type of action... Fuck it, desperate times...

I push the button for the trunk to open and I push started the car. As the shooter lit into the car I sprinted to the front of the car still in a crouch. Quickly raising up surprising the shooter once he stopped shooting I begin blazing through the trees. I caught him in the arm as he turned to run. Hearing the cops I chased him…

I might not be able to run a 4.1 anymore and I'm thicker than I was in high school but I'm still fast and in shape, but this bitch nigga was fast! Chasing him down the alley I let off more shots but they were wild ones. The shooter turned runner began to zig-zag and get small never losing speed.

"Damn!" I don't know how but this little nigga turned left and with his only good arm leapt over a fence. I wasn't doing that! No way, no how. So I stopped and aimed my pistol through the fence and squeeze off two quick shots. Again catching the shooter this time in the leg, causing him to let out a sound only being hit by hollow rounds can cause.

As he falls to the ground in somebody's back yard I climb the fence hearing sirens very close, too close if you ask me. Fifteen feet away I tell the shooter to stand and face me. Slowly he gets up and turns toward me.

"Pick up yo gun!" I yell at him.

Breathing hard and tired I stand ready. As soon as the shooter straightens up he begins to move his arm, gotta respect him, but he was too slow raising his gun, plus I doubt that he was left-handed. I shot 'em three times in the face.

I need to send a message to whoever was on my line and actions speak louder than words was the way I was taught!

Unlike before this time shit didn't go as easily. Killing somebody in someone else's backyard was a little messy and chasing him down don't really scream self-defense, "Ah my life in danger!"

Once a cop always a cop I told them. The Captain didn't like it so I stayed and listened to some threats and screams.

I dropped the glass off to my fingerprint guy and told him to hit me up ASAP. It's safe to say the Ridgewood crib isn't safe. In the future my loft might really have to be my home. I really don't like how that sounds. I really have to put this shit back in order. Don't like a muthafucka dictating where I live!

"Oh shit! This shit is lit! We about to win another chip!" Moose says coming into the kitchen. Everybody was in a good mood. Moose and Tots because the Pistons were about to bring another chip to the City, I was in a good mood because shit was finally feeling normal again. Pussy, money, and a shootout! Get into all three in a day, can't beat it.

Rev just left claiming it was too much testosterone with Moose in the house. The best thing is that nobody was asking about my almost being killed and that was the most important thing. Ever since I been back everybody been treating me like I'm fragile, and they didn't know half of what went on with Emilio. Wheeew, just imagine!

"Nigga don't say shit! I gotta show you something." Moose says all excited and nervous as she keep looking over her shoulder whispering. Obviously whatever it was she didn't want Tots to know about it. I think as she pulls out her phone, Moose shows me a video of Cherish fucking herself with a nice-sized dildo. Not say nothing but it's hard not to compare mother and daughter. Cherish is thicker but both have nice skin and pretty pussies. Cherish kept a landing strip on hers though and I see they both like to send videos, thinking of the one Ebony sent me this morning...

Cherish was really working the dildo. Now I couldn't help but compliment her on her body and the way she was sucking her juices off that dildo had me thinking about her and Clay. I was definitely getting moist from watching her show. Moose must've sensed it cause she ended the video before Cherish really got going. Moose was easily pussy whipped.

"So you fuckin' her?" I know it's a stupid question but I was trying to put shit together in my head. Because this was crazy!

"Yeah, we been fuckin' for a minute now. And Cuz, she a freak! Old bitch took me by surprise." Moose kept talking like she always do when she get to talking about pussy. She just like a nigga in so many ways... Damn Cherish fucking both Moose and the Mayor!

"Did she ever ask you about me?" I ask cutting Moose off because now I'm starting to wonder something.

"Yeah, she says she remembers us from when we used to hoop. I told her about you being a P.I. and shit. Did she contact you? She said she might, something about somebody stealing." I let Moose continue as I think. So that's how she found me. But why did she hired me? She had to know I'll find out about her fuckin' the Mayor. This shit was crazy. I was fucking Ebony, Tots is fucking Clay, and Moose is fucking Cherish. I'm starting to see that there's more to Cherish than I thought and I wouldn't be surprised if she was hip to all this. I had to be careful with her. She was on something else other than finding who Clay is fucking.

"So why you showing me and why you don't want Tots to see?" I ask, confused because they were so close.

"Man Cuz, I'm really feeling this old bitch and Tots just ended it with the Mayor. You know she pregnant and shit (shaking her head)... I want to know what you think. Am I tripping and should I tell Tots?" I look at her as she drinks her beer. Rev raised both of us together. Moose was like a sister to me. She was a year older than me but all of our lives she been girl crazy so I'm used to pulling her off the ledge.

"Well yeah! You tripping bout that old bitch and you gotta tell Tots! We don't keep secrets." I say even though I had no plans on telling them about me and Ebony.

"I'm gonna tell you something, Moose... Know I hate to tell you this, Cuz I..." I put my head down like it really hurt me to say the next words.

"Nigga what?!?" Moose yells.

"Cuz, I fucked Brittany! Ahhhh!!!" I yell in her face and run past her.....

Moose shared everything with us that night. Neither Tots nor I told her why Cherish really hired me and I didn't tell either of them about Cherish and the Mayor. Moose is tender dick, which made no sense to me since her dick was plastic.

ALL GOOD A WEEK AGO

My phone ringing wakes me outta my sleep causing me to nearly push Sara out the small bed we were laying in in Tots' spare room. Re-watching Cherish's video after the game had me calling Sara to stay the night with me. Plus I doubled back and sent a copy of the video of Cherish to myself. Never know, might come in handy later.

"Somebody just firebombed the Bar," Rev calmly says into my phone waking me up completely at 3:00am.

The scene wasn't that bad, a little cocktail bomb, something light. I felt bad because I knew it had something to do with me. I couldn't prove it, but I knew it, and Rev and Joyce knew it too.

With a cocktail bomb like this Rev and Joyce were in little harm, but this felt more like Emilio than anyone else. None of my recent cases felt like this. Today I was hoping to learn something from that glass. I got a strong feeling it would break shit wide open for me. Flex just didn't seem right to me. The Mayor case was getting odd but not dangerous.

"I'm sorry Pops... You know whatever the insurance don't cover I got you." I say hoping I can since my business was affected also, plus I was 100% responsible for this.

"You calling me Pops twice in one day?" Rev asked raising his eyebrows. "Think you getting soft on me Vegas these days." Smiling and throwing a jab.

"It's cool. The insurance should be able to cover this but me and Joyce won't be here. I'ma let you handle it."

"Whoa what? Where Joyce think she going? This job don't come with vacation!" I shout fake-serious as Joyce walks up after bossing the cops around.

"Dealing with you she earned it, and we going to Paris and you paying for the tickets!" Throwing his arms around Joyce's shoulders he guides her back toward the apartment.

"Round trip, first class!" Joyce yells over her shoulder leaving me looking crazy. They wake me up to leave me to handle this.

"It's life. I live it."

Later that morning after sending Rev and Joyce off, refusing my ride to the airport labeling my Charger as a target bulletproof or not, I sit at my Coney having breakfast and talking to Spokes about opening up a bike shop. I already had him a garage where he keeps his bikes and fixes them up. I don't know why but I been feeling motherly lately, probably being around Tots so much, raising her child is the only thing she talks about.

I guess it's only right that I push the little nigga to do something positive since I have him doing so much bullshit. Spokes was liking the idea and getting excited when all of the sudden a van pulls up braking loud as fuck!

I was fast on alert looking through the window. Pulling out both of my pistols I aim at the van as I stand. I tell Spokes to get down and I tell myself to shoot as soon as the doors open…

I didn't though because when the doors to the van slide open a girl came flying out in only her panties and bra. Before I could run for the door the van sped off. Looking toward the girl I didn't have to be a M.E. to know she was dead, but I did have to get closer to realize that the dead girl was Kitty and I was shocked! I pulled out my phone and took a few pictures of her before I left.

This shit makes no sense! First the Holy Water gets cocktailed and hours later Kitty's dead body gets thrown from a van in front of Coney. MY Coney at that! Are both incidents connected? I don't know, but I was headed to the police station to find out about those prints.

With shit heating up it was good Rev and Joyce were leaving now, less I have to worry about. I can afford to be a little reckless. It sounds wrong but Kitty being dead was also a good thing. Truthfully the case was now closed and I can focus more attention on who put that ticket on my head but finding who Flex is, is first priority though.

ALL GOOD A WEEK AGO

CHAPTER 9

Back when I was on the force, my little two and a half years, I spent most of it undercover. I built some strong relationships with some cops who was willing to play fair with the other side. My fingerprints guy Miles was one of those cops. I was now sitting at his desk looking around the open office and it was noisy! This floor being shared by Homicide and Robbery. Cops sat in less than comfortable chairs talking loudly into phones or to each other. I got more than a few hated looks. Trust me, most cops didn't like me, they were positive that some of their unsolved cases were caused by me in one way or another. Some still wonder how I was a cop for two and a half years and never arrested anyone. I never had an answer to that. At times like this I think back when I gave back my badge I give credit to Rev for that.

Before I turned my badge in I went to talk to Rev and he asked me how I felt. At first I didn't understand the question. Then he asked me to pull out my badge and he repeated the question. It was crazy because the only times I felt uncomfortable were whenever I had my badge on around Rev or whenever I was in the police station with other cops. The only time I actually felt undercover was when I was around other cops. That day I told Rev that and like always he joked but I knew there was some truth to it when he quoted the line from "In Too Deep," "You ain't no cop J Reed, you ain't no cop!" Rev was joking but it was true, and I knew it. I think everybody did too and that's why it was so easy for the streets to embrace me back. Don't get it twisted. I did put in my work!

I still have to say I was more than happy when Miles dropped a file as he perched on the edge of the desk.

"That's the file on the person whose fingerprints were on that glass." I thought it was thin as I picked it up. I was more surprised that the prints belonged to RaQuan Fowler! Holding my composure and hoping Miles couldn't see how furious I was or stupid I felt.

"A gun charge, that's his only case huh?" When I looked up at Miles I was shaking inside.

"As far as Michigan goes. I only checked our database. Do you know him?"

"Yeah, I used to. Thanks Miles, I gotta go. I owe you one. As a matter of fact I'll have Spokes drop it off to you." I say as I get up no longer caring how I looked or sounded. This was proof I was slipping bad and I was planning to take it out on this nigga when I catch him.

Hopping into my Charger I text Flex AKA Fat Cat Quan! I text him the picture of Kitty's dead body and tell him the case was closed. He didn't know I knew who he was and I was positive the bitch nigga is the one who put the hit on my head.

Still a little confused at what game he's playing, because it makes no sense he had at least two chances to kill me himself. Little does he know the game that he's playing just got dangerous for him! I call Tots and Moose and tell them to meet me on Ridgewood. Not feeling as vulnerable as I once was knowing it was a bitch nigga like Quan gunning for me.

"But why is he trying to be a bitch tho?" Moose asks.

For the last 30 minutes I been putting them in the loop about the Kitty case. We all have come to the conclusion that Kitty wasn't his niece. Moose's last question was just one of the few that had us fucked up. It's easy to understand why he wanted me killed, but why he didn't do it when he had multiple chances?

"He went through a lot of trouble for nothing!" Tots says as she takes her shoes off and lay on my couch. That's a pregnant bitch for you.

"But why he want to be a bitch?" Moose asks again and I could see the confusion on her face as she looks at the picture of Flex from our first meeting that a waitress got for me.

"I done partied with the nigga, he likes hoes. Come on, you remember the nigga Mags, man!"

"Maybe being fucked by Boots made him feel some type of way. Fucked up his psyche." Tots says sounding like a psychiatrist. As she and Moose continue to question Quan's psyche I'm thinking about how I'm going to get to this nigga. One thing was for sure though, when I do get Quan unlike him I'm not playing. It's gonna be 5 head shots!

Information plays a big part in what I do. It's how I get money from these niggas so easy and it's why people come to me when their shit come up missing, I know things. Quan should know this. He should know I still know where his mom and his two daughters live. He should know I have no problem using them to get to him... No problem! My phone starts vibrating and I see it's Gage at 10:30pm, this got to be important.

"Vegas, this Gage." Duh, Gage always do this like caller ID was never invented.

"I'm still following the Mayor and now he's at Belle Isle and he been parked here for like 10 minutes. Right now he's talking to his wife. Don't ask how I know. He's informing her he'll be out later than usual. To my knowledge he's alone in the car. I got a feeling you might want to be here because in the movies these type of meetings be important."

What the fuck! The Mayor is cheating, that's it! Gage acts like the Mayor is out here making dope moves. This case is bullshit...

"Vegas, Vegas! You still there?"

"Yeah, I'm just thinking." I say sounding bored and tired of this case which is far from my usual type of work.

"Okay, I'll be there and stay alert. I'm coming on foot so don't shit yo self when I slide on you." Gage began talking again but I end the call. Following cheating husbands just doesn't hold my attention especially when muthafuckas shooting at me. But like I said information is money. Late night meeting in the park with a cheating husband sounds like sex to me but you never know what the Mayor might be into. Detroit's Mayors have a history of having their hands dirty…

If being shot at and then having the nigga who put a hun bun on your head in front of you and you not know doesn't make you more alert then man… you deserve to be killed!

So of course I notice the blue van following me. I was doing 25 mph down Grand River, nothing out of the norm, I didn't want to alert them I was hip. I was so happy to be back in my Charger where I can use voice command.

"Call Ball." See this my City and whoever is following me is about to find that out. After talking to Short Fuse ain't no telling who this nigga is or where he from, so now every time I kill one of these clowns I was seeing it as me doing it for the City. Can't have niggas coming from all over taking hits in the City!

"Vegas! It's been a minute. Boy Boy came through, Friday I'll have that for you." This morning I had Spokes drop a brick of dog food and half a brick of that fetty to Ball. One of my low key niggas from Vandyke.

"That's cool, but I'm thinking why give me anything?" Looking in my rearview I see the van is three cars back. I was pushing 30 mph now.

"Ah shit, put me in the game coach!" I can hear the excitement in Ball's voice. I understand why because Rev said the shit I finessed Jssiah out of was potent. Had me wondering how Jssiah got plugged in where he can get it that pure.

"How fast can you get two niggas at the corner of Warren and Charmers? With A.R.'s…"

"What! In minutes!"

ALL GOOD A WEEK AGO

"I'm turning down West Warren now. Be there in like 7 minutes. I'm being followed by a blue van. When I stop at the light put holes in that bitch for me!"

"Say no more!" Keeping my speed at 35 mph I hit a few corners with the van still two cars back. No doubt I think if I wasn't in my bulletproof Charger they would've lit my ass up by now.

I was passing the juvenile court house when the van moved to a car behind me. I was still a ways from Charmers... I continue like I'm clueless to their presence as I kept it at 30 mph driving down Forest.

A light from Charmers I move in front of a car I was trying to keep at least one car between us I had to slow down, East Warren is always more busy than West Warren. I could've chosen any block in the City but East Warren is always hot and since I'm petty whenever I get the chance to make it hotter I take it.

My mind was already made up that no matter green or red I was stopping regardless. I look around as I approach Charmers to see if I could peep Ball's shooters and to my surprise I see Ball himself posted as I stop at the light. Glad to see Ball I like the type of nigga who make sure shit gets done right. I hit my signal indicating that I'm turning just as two shooter walk up to the van out of the blue. They did it so smooth that they had me wondering where they came from...

THUDTUDTUDUDUDUDUD.. THUDTUDUD!

Man this shit sounded like a helicopter was starting up, that's the only way I could describe the sound. I been in many shootouts but never have I heard anything like this. Whoever was in that van had no chance, but they had no chance the moment they started following me. Just like that it was over and I was making my turn and heading toward Belle Isle.

There was something that stood out to me as odd. I don't know if it was shock or because we in Detroit are so used to shootings, but when they were letting them A.R.'s off not one car skirt off and no one panicked and caused an accident. That made me think of a Jay-Z line and like always I had to quote it, "They say we are prone to violence/ But it's home sweet home/ where personalities clash and chrome meet chrome."

"Yo necessito el contacto que yo te pague much dinero Alcalde Church… Pero por favor dime que tu vida no teene un precio de tres milliones de dollars."

Sitting in Gage's Camry, how this nigga is still alive is a wonder. I am parked five cars down from the Mayor. If Clay was looking up he probably saw me opening this clown car door since the fool had his interior lights on. It's not like you see people with two pistols in shoulder holsters walking around.

This meeting did seem strange now that I was here and looking at the few pictures that Gage took. It was of some Spanish dude. He looked Puerto Rican or Dominican and was well-dressed. Listening to him talk to the Mayor his tone said enough, even if I didn't speak Spanish, but I would have never known this.

"I need that contact, I paid you a lot of money Mayor Church… But please tell me your life don't have a two million dollar price tag on it…" If that wasn't a threat! Judging by his look in the picture and tone on the audio whoever this man was he was serious.

"Junito come on! You worry too much. This is my city, I said you got the contract then they are yours… this is not Puerto Rico or the D.R. This type of project takes time… If you want your money back, that's a snap of the finger! But what you need to remember is that I chose you and not the other way around. Your threat, although serious I'm sure, means nothing!" Whatever Clay got himself into it was clear he could handle it. Hearing Clay more so than his words made me smile, call it City pride. Just like I couldn't let muthafuckas from outta town shoot at me and get away. Clay can't let muthafuckas think they can come here and run shit either! I mean that's how I see it. More important though is that this case was starting to talk money to me! Information is knowledge, and knowledge is everything!

"So what you think they got going on with that contract stuff?" It's obvious and in the near future this information will be worth a mil or two.

"Gage…" I say putting my head down realizing that Gage could speak Spanish too and that was putting me in a difficult situation. "Gage what you just hard was the Mayor selling City contracts. I don't know what this contract is, but I will." Learning what this contract talk was all about was on my to do list.

"But it's important… Now I'm gonna have to take you off the case and you can go."

"Come on Vegas, don't take me off this case!" Gage says cutting me off and hearing him whine like that really reminded me how young he was. Now 19 and in his sophomore year at Wayne State he was like a little brother to me. I been supporting him since he was 13 after we watched his mother overdose. It was hard for me to show it, but in my own way I loved him as much as Moose, Tots, or Joyce. I so much want to be a part of his success.

"Gage this shit too dangerous now! This type of money they talking… Just knowing this info can get you killed. I don't want that shit on my conscience!" It wasn't many people I loved, but Gage was one of those people. I have him doing jobs just to give him money. Now that he's grown I felt it made him feel like a man, but I never believed I ever put him in real danger and I didn't plan to now.

"Now forget what you heard here and get you ass back on campus!" Rev is probably right that I'm getting soft, before I'm not sure I would've cared, but who knows. Tricks and I hop out of Gage's car once the Mayor and his partner pull off with plans to meet some females.

For the last two days Tricks been with Gage. He likes having her around when he's on one of these jobs for me. Although I believe Quan is behind the Hundred Thousand ticket on my head it's still not for sure. So I can get Quan out the way and still be gunned at… Crazy but I can't keep this smile off my face now I'm thinking about Clay leaving Ebony alone… Shiiiit what's to think about!

CHAPTER 10

Friday morning I'm in my Charger in the Coney drive thru… Shid, I'm not stupid! Muthafuckas ain't getting a easy kill. (chuckling) Funny Flex A.K.A. Quan hasn't hit me back since I sent him a picture of Kitty. I just text him telling him I'm trying to link up and if he wants I can find the killers of his niece. I put Tots and Moose on Quan's truck so I'm expecting to have my pistol in his mouth soon. Now that the Mayor's case is showing dolla signs I'm more anxious to close this and get into that.

Back in the day Quan used to be seen heavy in Highland Park or around here. I was hoping I'd get a glance and a shot at Quan. I'm cruising down Woodward heading to his Mom's crib. After last night I doubt I'll be followed again but old habits die hard I'm told, so I still hit a few corners just to make sure.

"Ms. Fowler, excuse me. May I have a word with you?" I say after hopping out of my Charger. I was dressed in running gear this sunny morning. White leggings and a matching sports bra with my Air Max Nikes.

Quan's mom was sitting on her porch looking like Martin Lawrence's version of Big Momma. Seeing a woman with two pistols hanging under her arms I could only imagine what she was thinking as I stood in her face.

"Who the hell is you! And why you want a word with me?" It's clear this was no Big Momma and here I was trying to sound nice.

"I'm a friend of your son Quan. I heard he was back in the city, I was hoping he was here."

"Humph... If he's back I haven't seen him and to my knowledge his daughters haven't either and I don't care. So if that's why you stopped by you can go about your way now." After that she waved me off and went back to her puzzle. She must not have heard what DMX said... man that woman crazy I think as I hop back in my car and pull out my phone to take a pic. At least Quan was smart enough not to come around his family looking like that.

"Put me in position!" Not hiding my excitement as I answer the phone for Tots.

"Nigga bitch, chill. I pulled that truck over and it was only one nigga in it. Dark skin nigga wit dreads... Sound familiar?"

"Yeah, that's one of his goons. Gee I think that's his name." Damn I was hoping they'll catch Quan and get this shit over with.

"Cuff him and take him to Rich Tony's blood spot I was telling you and Moose about." I knew Rich Tony was outta town so we should be good. "Leave his keys under the front seat." Another job for Spokes.

To bring less attention I parked a block away and left my pistols in the car, I was feeling so naked. I played the alleys to Rich Tony's spot with crowbar in hand. I came into his spot from the back door stepping into the dining room I see Moose punching Gee with a straight right/left combo. Tape across his mouth muffling his scream.

"Yeah nigga! I told you in the car this shit was going to get ugly for you!" Moose spit massaging her hands.

"What's this about Tots?"

"Yo crazy ass cousin being crazy. This fool thinking he was going to the precinct so he start talking crazy. Country ass didn't know how we get down up here."

Moose had Gee wrapped in chains the same way I imagine Rich Tony had Corn in this room days ago. Damn what a week this been. Gee was held up by a chain hanging from the ceiling through his neck collar. Moose's idea I bet.

I begin walking toward him dragging the crowbar across the wood floor. Once I was in range I cock my arm all the way back taking a big swing at Gee's kneecap.

BLOC!

Gee instantly drops and the sound from the crowbar meeting knee blocks out the sound of his knee breaking. Gee stays on the floor obviously in pain damn near choking himself being cuffed and wrapped in chains completely powerless. I always believe it's better to start with violence and allow whoever on the other end of that violence to convince you not to continue.

"Tots, fill the tub and Moose pull this country boy up, but put the chain through the leg braces." I pick up Gee's phone and look through it. I know there's some important shit I can find in it but I'm so geeked I can't focus. I go to the kitchen and grab a chair for Tots; her being pregnant and all.

Hanging upside down I had to crouch down to look Gee in the eye. Looking like a man who knows he's in some shit. I was happy to see that.

"Gee, don't scream at all!!" Hoping my point was clear and he could decipher the look in my eyes as I pulled the tape from across his mouth.

"I got some questions…" I told Gee as he was paying more attention to Moose even though I was the one who hit him with the crowbar. See this is what I'm talking about. I nod to Moose and she takes aim and kicks Gee in the ribs. Like always she was wearing Tims.

"Ahh, shit! HU hun…"

"Now Gee, why Flex in my City?" Using the name Flex not knowing if Gee knew Flex's real name. Gee takes his time still trying to breathe and get used to the pain. I know his broken knee is killing him.

"All I know is he's obsessed with you. You probably can't tell but he's crazy." I nod to Moose again and she lowers Gee until his head is chin deep in cement muffling his scream…

"Tu, tis, tisk… Fuck! Why you do that fo?" Gee spit cement from his mouth and yells at me.

"How long was he in Atlanta and what was he doing there?" Gee takes his time glaring at me. I nod to Moose who's smiling.

"Okay okay!" Ignoring his plea I tell Moose to dip him again. This time for 20 seconds.

I wait patiently and think as Gee shakes most of the cement from his face. This nigga Quan is up to something. He wants me dead, not just because of what I had Boots do to him. Nah… He wants to move freely in the City and he knew at the end of the day I would've learned who Flex really was.

"He been down there for years moving drugs, and he a part time owner of this magazine. You know Flex fit right in down there, you know, wit him looking like that. But he ain't got shit on them Trans down there, feel me. Plus he don't really fuck wit niggas, feel me. So them freaks down there didn't embrace him for real, feel me… But he had the best drugs and prices, feel me." Gee says that last part like this was the reason he was working for Quan. But I wasn't feeling this nigga at all, feel me? (Chuckling to myself)

"Where is he?"

"I don't know, nobody seen him since he killed Kitty… You know that wasn't his niece, feel me. He called BJ yesterday, feel me, now he gone too, feel me. If you let me go I'ma leave yo City and go back to the 'A'… promise!"

"What do you mean he's crazy?" I start pacing. I'll hate to be trying to find a crazy nigga. Ain't no telling what a real crazy nigga might do or be.

"He crazy like I said, feel me. One minute he's talking bout he hate you and gon' kill you. A minute later he telling us how smart and beautiful you is, feel me. Saying how you inspire him. Crazy,

crazy. One minute he only fuckin' Kitty and later he calling me to fuck him. Crazy crazy, feel me." Gee starts shaking his head trying to stop the cement from going into his eyes.

"Damn! Vegas, you really fucked that nigga up." Tots says and I had to agree with her. This shit strange I'm thinking as I try to put the tape back across Gee's mouth I tell Moose to dip him. Perfect, we leave Gee hanging upside down shoulder deep in the cement-filled tub. It was two in the afternoon. I'll have Spokes set the house on fire around 8:00pm tonight. I hope Rich Tony got insurance.

If you in Detroit and looking for somebody like Quan A.K.A. Flex you gotta drive through Palmer Park. The most comfortable place for the LGBT and all them other alphabets. It's not that I hate that community, I just hate that they trying too hard to be accepted. Fuck that! I'm a lesbian, you don't like it? Try me! Fuck trying to get a law passed, if you can't protect yourself well then you fucked!

Anyways, Palmer Park ain't all LGBT, it's straight people too of course. One nigga I fuck with who been getting money over there forever taking advantage of the fact that most niggas not trying to be around that bullshit. My nigga Ant was the nigga in these parks hands down. I'm not here to say the nigga don't fuck around, I don't know… Pulling up in front of his apartments I see a few niggas around him. Ant's black ass was sitting in a lawn chair cracking jokes on some young ass nigga as I step up.

"What the fuck! My nigga!" Ant stands up after saying that, obviously surprised to see me. Like I said, I been outta action but he was putting a ten on it. I still clap hands and tell him to walk with me…

"Ant I'm looking for a nigga and I know he had to come through here and if he had then he had to see you." I hand my phone to him and show him a picture of Flex… Ant look up at me and I know he's seen Flex. I know Ant can read my expression and he knows I ain't fucking around.

"Damn Vegas… Even though I want to I ain't gon lie… Man… yeah he been through here a couple times." The way Ant is acting I'm positive Quan offered him a crazy deal on some work.

"You talked to him then?" I roughly put my arm around Ant's shoulder as we walk; we are about the same height but he was wider by far in the shoulders.

"Ah, man…" Ant shakes his head. "Yeah we talked. The nigga name is Flex, he from the A. Nigga got his hands on everything! Vegas you fucking my shit up." I can't believe this nigga just said that, how quick we forget, huh?

"What! You don't know what I want with him… What he asked about me?"

"Nah, he just seem like a nigga trying to move some work. You know I do my thang and I been working this area since I was 11. That's 20 years. I got crack houses, Boy houses, weed houses, and pill houses. But this nigga the real deal gonna put me in position to be moving bricks through the City." Ant stopped and smiled a sad smile at me.

"Nigga I can't believe you running yo resume by me like I don't know! You for real right now!"

"But Vegas we go waaay back so fuck him, like they used to say cut me in or cut it out." Ant was right we did some big shit back in the day, but he just fucked up in so many ways because you can't shake me down and I wasn't believing him at all. I smile at Ant. He don't even know his time as being the nigga around here was coming to an end.

"Nigga you ain't said nothing, play yo part you know I look out for mine. Next time he pull up hit my hip and clear out." I heard all I needed to hear to let me know that Ant wasn't fucking with me…

I wonder if Quan ever had plans of revealing himself to anyone. He was smart to try and use Ant as the front man of his operation. I can't speak for any other city, but here in Detroit a muthafucka like Flex could never be respected in these streets.

Brittany's fine high yellow ass was standing above me while I lay on my bed naked at my Ridgewood house. Slowly rolling her slim hips to some new song from Queen Nija. Her big stupid sloppy pussy lips glisten. Goddamn! I'm in the mood where I just want to eat some pussy! She didn't have the prettiest pussy but Brittany's shit smelled and tasted sooo good it was dazzling. I haven't ate a pussy that wasn't addictive so that goes without saying, but thank you God for pussy I think as she lowers herself inviting me to heaven!

After multiple sips from the fountain of Brittany, and as good as it was, I'll be lying if I say I wasn't happy to see her go. In this way I guess I'm more like a nigga than a bitch, but I just needed to be alone and have a chance to think. I had all the lights off throughout the house and I was soaking in the tub with all my lavender scented candles on. With a blunt in one hand a pistol in the other, I felt like I left one heaven for another. Of course my mind drifted to Quan. I'm no psych. But I can understand the damage I caused. Brittany said she still hadn't heard from Cherry. Damn it, if Quan met up with her stupid ass she's probably dead depending on what type of mood you catch him in. Thinking about it I can see his obsession with me showing with the tats and the piercings. Shit, I don't know why he hasn't answered my calls. Our showdown is inevitable. Right now I can rub my pussy and cum from the thought of putting five in his head if only for the reason he thought he could be me.

CHAPTER 11

What the fuck was this nigga's problem, I think as I sit on my porch eating a bowl of Trix going through my phone. Earlier I saw that Gage sent me pictures of Clay and Junito from two nights ago. I know I told that lil punk to go back to campus that night and that this case was over for him! For the last hour I have been trying to get ahold of him. He and Sara both go to Wayne State, so I called her. She said she hadn't seen him in a couple days on campus. With all this shit going on Gage picked the wrong time to not listen to me. Since he's older now I guess I'll have to reestablish who I represent in our relationship. Later I'll slide up on his ass, but today I decided when I woke up that I'll put a little pressure on Quan, get him to come out of hiding. First thing though, I gotta get dressed and pull up on Tots.

The other day when Tots and Moose picked up Quan's guy Gee I had Spokes drive Gee's truck to my Ridgewood house and park it in my garage. So on this sunny day around noon that's what I'm in instead of my Charger. I had Moose check to see if it was reported stolen or anything and it wasn't so I was feeling very low-key in this. I was starting to think that Quan really didn't care about the dudes he brought up here from Atlanta. As I see it he was sacrificing them like pawns.

Dressed in gym shorts and a Grant Hill jersey to match my Grant Hills I was feeling very comfortable and safe with my bullet proof vest on under my jersey. As always my two 9's were at my ribcage. I was definitely in my comfort zone as I turned off Plymouth and down Steel headed for Tots' crib.

"Nigga bitch just don't be letting yourself in unannounced!" Tots fake snap on me seeing me laid out on her couch going through a magazine. She was coming fresh out of the shower. Her towel was still wrapped around her body. The smell of soap was coming off her body. She always had a thing for raspberry scented fragrances and right now she was smelling tasty! Tots had a glow to her. I don't know if it was from the shower or if she was rocking a pregnant woman glow. Anyway, she was looking good, even better than usual.

"Tots cut it out you knew it was me. You eat something?"

"Nah."

"Go get dressed and I'll make you an omelet, pregnant ass getting fat!"

"What you for real? I asked you the other day, you said I wasn't showing!" She wasn't, but she been asking me non-stop. I don't know if she's disappointed that she wasn't showing or relieved, being only three weeks pregnant I don't know what she expected. I'm starting to notice that ever since I learned that she was pregnant I been seeing Tots in a different way. I'm surprised how easy it was for me to see her as a fragile person. All this time we been friends I'm positive that I never cooked for her or brought her a chair. What's also surprising is how easily she accepted me treating her like that...

"You know this guy?" I ask Tots once she was done eating two omelets and three slices of toast. The guy in the picture was Junito, he was with Clay.

"Nah, I never seen him. But I... wait! You don't think Clay and him fucking!? Cause I know for sure."

ALL GOOD A WEEK AGO

"Whoa, chill!" I yell to cut her off taking my phone from her. I find the audio from that night and I let Tots listen to it... Once the audio was over I asked Tots what she thought. She was on his detail and I was hoping she had some clue to this project.

"I don't know what contract he's talking about, but the biggest contract that's up for bid is the Belle Isle one." I must've had a what the fuck you talking about look on my face.

"Vegas, stop playing! Where the fuck you be at and doing all day? Nigga bitch, they talking about turning Belle Isle into something crazy, more than just a park." I was still lost.

"What the fuck you talking about?"

"I heard Clay on the phone explaining it, well more like Cherish was explaining it to him. Some big time person or company was paying Detroit 3 billion to buy Belle Isle, with the plan to collaborate with the City Chosen developer to build and design certain parts or whatever. I don't know all the in's and out's of the deal, but it's supposed to bring a lot of money into the city."

"3 billion, man! What the fuck is he planning on turning Belle Isle into? And bitch you expected me to know this?" Bitch knows I'm from the streets. Shit, Clay was only one of the four mayors I could name and I'm sure we had more in my twenty-seven years.

"Vegas this shit been going on for the whole time Clay was running and been the biggest topic since he been Mayor. Shit it was the big thing he ran on, he promised to bring more money to the city and clean up the neighborhoods and their surrounding parks." There she go sounding like she was in love with the nigga, bitch act like I wasn't on an Emilio vacation! But I'm not going to point that out.

"Damn, bitch you sound like you in love with the nigga."

"Not at all! Nigga I was just putting yo ignorant ass in the loop!" Tots says going through the pictures of Clay and Junito again.

"Vegas, 2 million not nearly enough to buy this contract." Yeah from the way she made this contract sound and me being a professional extortionist, shiit I could take no less than 30 million.

"Yeah Tots you know what you know. There's probably more to this deal."

"You Google his name? Nigga not that much of a mystery that Google don't know his ass!" Tots asked and I look at her wondering do she feel some type of way since Clay was the sperm donor of her child.

"Tots shut up, you know us not having his name it's gonna take all day. Shiit, we don't know shit about the muthafucka!" Time like this I wonder how she made detective.

"You know what Tots? I was thinking, you should take a vacation. You know, the maternal leave or whatever." When I say this I make sure I'm sitting eye to eye with her so she knows I'm serious. Things was only going to get worse and if Quan was trying to hurt me going through Tots could be an option. Being a cop didn't mean she wasn't untouchable. I'd be lying if I didn't say her being pregnant didn't play a big part in me worrying about her. Lord knows she was well-prepared to take care of herself in normal times, or maybe I'm getting soft!

"Nigga bitch chill! I'm not even showing yet, plus I was already planning to go visit Ma in Dallas when I get like two months." Tots and her mother were very close. As a matter of fact all three of us were close to her and we all call her Ma. A few years ago she got married and she moved to Dallas. Tots having plans to visit her already told me a lot but waiting wasn't going to work. I'll let it go for the moment, but I had plans to stay on her about that. I stayed with Tots for a minute trying to figure out a way to learn who Junito was. Even while doing this my mind wasn't too far from Quan.

Driving down McNichoals heading toward Palmer Park, years ago like 7 to be exact, there was a dude named Paul a.k.a. Pusha P or Palmer P, clown had all types of names. Well he supplied that area, he even had Ant buying from him. Paul is only 8 years older than us but back then he had a strong hold on the drug game in Palmer Park. That was until several robberies for a month straight non-stop his drug spots was getting robbed and Paul was never able to recover from that, at least he never got his top spot back.

ALL GOOD A WEEK AGO

Out of the blue Ant popped up with a small plug on everything and took over Palmer Park overnight it seemed. I'm thinking it's time to return the power to Pusha P or whatever name he's going by nowadays. That's my thought as I hit a few blocks looking for Paul.

I was in the parking lot on the far end away from the basketball court, Gee had limo tint on all his windows and I had them up. From here I could easily see Ant's apartment and like most times he and his guys were posted. I could be wrong but more than likely Any noticed this truck as Quan's a.k.a. Flex. More than once I saw him staring down this way. I find it strange that he, as in Quan, hasn't called Gee's phone or answered when I called him from this phone. Not that surprising seeing as how he's used his pawns so far...

"Yes Ms. Towns," Answering Cherish's question if this was the only time I caught the mayor with another woman. I was only showing her the few pictures I had with the mayor and the female, none with Junito. On my way over I was contemplating if I should bring up Junito or not. One of my rules is to never give up valuable information for free. If the mayor was into something illegal, which he was, tipping him I was hip to this information too early could lose me some easy money. Worse, it could be putting me in some danger I'm not prepared for. This Junito character could be more dangerous than Emilio. That thought was not a welcoming one.

"I know it's been a few days, believe me I been on him the whole time. I know you believe he's cheating but this is all I got on him. If you want... I'll continue to follow him." Cherish had her back to me and we were back in the same room as last time. Sitting here I was wondering now where she recorded that video for Moose. The way her pencil skirt was hugging her hips was causing me to have mental snap shots of her chocolate ass.

"This was from two nights ago, right? The Mayor had a late meeting that night. Did you see who the Mayor was having that meeting with?" Cherish never took her eyes off me when she asked this. She had me feeling like she knew the answer already but I had no reason to lie about seeing Junito.

"Of course I seen who he was with. Bu-ut since it wasn't a woman I thought nothing of it. Oh wait! Should I… What! You think the Mayor?!?" I raised my eyebrows and hoped Cherish got the idea. Already getting it from Tots that the Mayor was far from gay I was throwing this out there hoping to throw Cherish off on how much I was interested in the Mayor and Junito's relationship.

Cherish chuckled. "No, no!" She waved me off. "No Vegas, the Mayor isn't gay. That just was an important meeting, one that shouldn't get out to the public." Cherish stared at me with a strange look that was hard for me to decipher. Picking up her purse she asked me if I needed more money to continue the case. I was still trying to figure out what Cherish's intentions were. I accepted his case with the belief I was getting free money since I knew beforehand at least one woman the Mayor was cheating with. Now I'm feeling at some point soon I'm going to have to look into Cherish and find if there was a different reason she wanted me following Clay. With this on my mind I was a little slow to respond but I wasn't stupid, shiit! I took another fifteen hundred dollars before I left.

A couple hours later Moose, Paul, me and a few Dexter Boys met up at a strip mall on Division. I was trying to get my face back with the Dexter Boys after the Jssiah situation. The lick on Ant won't be anywhere near as much dope or money as the Jssiah lick would've been but only I knew it was never gonna really be a Jssiah lick. After this though my face should still be good. Being vouched for in every hood is important with me. I feel safe believing that if it's a nigga that's gunning for me there's at least one nigga who will put me in the loop. That's why Ant had to go. He was that one nigga in this area I believed I could count on. I don't know if he was hip to Quan a.k.a. Flex's intentions concerning me, but at this point I didn't care. To me my trust in him was gone, he fucked that up when he didn't hit my hip ASAP once Quan approached him.

It's no secret that Ant likes to spend a lot of time at the basketball court in Palmer Park. He really played the part of The Nigga around here, hosting big games and cookouts throughout the summer. So around eight that night it was damn near a ghost town in front of Ant's apartments when I slid in his building followed by Moose and Paul minutes later.

An hour later we were still waiting in Ant's two bedroom apartment. After searching every room we found little, but that wasn't surprising. Ant most likely had his money at the crib and his dope stashed in one of these apartments in the building. He probably has an apartment in one of these dope fiend names. Crazy, they out living on the streets or in somebody else's basement not know this nigga got an empty apartment stashing his little dope in.

Hearing voices in the hallway Moose steps back into the closet next to the door. Paul backed up in the bathroom door behind him and I stepped into the bedroom with a pistol grip double barrel sawed off shotgun. All of us were dressed in black, purposely I didn't tell Paul to wear gloves. I doubt if he noticed that he was the only one bare handed. He was too focused on getting his spot back from Ant. He wasn't doing too bad… His bag wasn't as big as it once was, but I think the big thing that had him heated was that he was now buying his work from Ant and not the other way around. The worst of it was that I knew that Ant sold him bullshit dope.

"Yeah, I'm in the crib now." I hear Ant say sounding like he was on the phone. I was hoping he was alone because this wasn't a robbery in the sense of taking Ant's cash, and the likelihood of anybody other than Moose, Paul, and me walking outta here was ZERO! Ant was still talking while walking into his bathroom. I assumed, because I didn't hear him for a minute before hearing the toilet flush. That's when I stepped out of the bedroom with the shotgun raised. I see Moose standing with her chrome pistol aimed down the hallway too. This was far from our first mission together and in times like these our minds were linked. I wished Tots was here… Ant stepped out of the bathroom and turned towards me and froze seeing my smile. I know he wished he didn't end that call. I nod causing him to look toward Moose.

"At least you washed yo hands nigga!" Hearing Moose's voice Paul stepped out of the bathroom and lightly tap Ant on the head with his pistol surprising Ant more.

"Yeah nigga," Paul said with his raspy voice. Finally finding his voice Ant asked me what this is about as Paul and I direct him back into the front room. Knowing that Ant knew me well I really wasn't concerned with him trying anything, at least not right now.

"Bitch nigga stop right there and keep them hands up!" Moose tell Ant before he got too close to her, sounding like a real cop. I tell Paul to put away his gun and pat Ant down. Moose and I with guns was enough. Too many guns out and something could go wrong.

"AH SHIT! Ahhh come on!" Ant yells when Moose punches him out the chair then kicked him in his stomach. Instead of Ant telling us where his dope and money was he just kept asking why we was robbing him. I had the Dexter Boys on the line ready to kick a door or two in. Before Ant could say something else Moose kicked him square in the face causing teeth and blood to fly everywhere!

Ever since I could remember Moose loved punishing niggas who had the odds stacked against them. I'm sure some doctor could find a reasonable explanation for this but I grew up with her and there wasn't one. But like every time before, we got what we was asking for. I made sure to tell the Dexter Boys not to kill Ant's B.M. or kids. Like I thought, Ant had his drugs in an empty apartment a floor down.

"Damn Vegas… You wrong for this after- after all the shit we don did. You do me like this?" Ant says this between the tears while trying to stop the blood that's leaking from his mouth looking up at me, looking like the bitch nigga he is. He wasn't in no way pulling at my heart strings with his performance. I was just hoping Paul was taking notes because one day this could be him if he ever forgot what went down.

"Bitch nigga shut the fuck up before I kick the rest of yo teeth out!" Moose snaps at Ant while at the same time backhanding the shit out of him.

"Years ago... Tell Paul who robbed him. What, three time Paul?" Paul stand there looking pissed. You can tell he was remembering his fall.

"Come on Vegas, don't do this. Please!" Ant doesn't even look up as he sits on the floor looking as pathetic as I ever seen a nigga.

"You want Moose to kick yo shit in again?"

"Naw man... I robbed you all three times." Paul quickly stepped over to Ant and start pistol-whipping him. The whole time Ant was yelling that I helped him before Moose pulled Paul off him.

"Paul, you hear that? I helped him rob you, I gave him his plug, I made this nigga!" I yell pointing at Ant who's laying on the floor crying in pain. I turn my back to him knowing that Moose had eyes on him.

"Like I told you earlier, I can put you back on top but being disloyal will get you killed with me." I didn't care how Paul felt about the role I played in his fall, but I wanted him to understand the role I'd play in his death if he decided to play by his rules and not mine. I tell Paul to hold the shotgun as I pick up Ant's phone.

I sent Paul and Moose away telling Moose to give Paul that other brick of boy and that brick and a half of fetty I still had from Jssiah. Plus I gave him those 3,000 pills I took off Bluff.

"Naw, Flex, this not Ant. It's me... Vegas." I say into the phone once Flex picks up thinking it's Ant. Quan answering for Ant's and not Gee's calls says a lot.

"Or should I call you Quan?" Ant look up instantly hearing that name. Before he moved Quan spent a lot of time in this area. "What? You thought I wouldn't find out?" I yell into the phone. Ant was sitting up in a chair cleaning his face with a rag. I guess he felt more comfortable with only me in the apartment.

"Vegas, what the fuck you want?"

"I wanna talk. Let's meet up, we can talk about the ticket you put on my head or BITCH we can talk about Big Black! You remember that?!?" As Quan cusses me out telling me what he is going to do to me when he gets his hands on me, I direct Ant to lay on the floor. I see the slight hesitation. I was ready... But a sheep is a sheep.

"If you going do all that let's meet up again and get it over with, bitch nigga. I know you want to be me."

"Vegas trust and believe we going to meet up again and this time it's gonna be you getting fucked in the ass." Quan says with a little bitch giggle. His easy transition from talking shit in a man's voice to the giggle was sick mix with crazy.

"How about here?" I ask as I send the picture I took of his mom on her front porch.

"HA! Bitch you wanna play!" Quan yells into the phone seconds later he sends me a picture of Cherry naked chained up like a dog clearly crying while eating cat food in front of an actual cat. Any other time it would've been funny and even though I didn't feel like it was my responsibility to save her but knowing he was treating a woman like this it did add fuel to my fire.

"Bitch nigga I don't give a fuck about her! You stupid!" I doubt it mattered to Quan if his actions affected me or not. What he was doing to Cherry he did to please himself.

"Yeah bitch, you care! But you be careful Vegas I'll be in touch." Quan ended the call and left me heated. I pocketed the phone.

"Ant you brought this on yo self... We had a nice thing going."

"Please Vegas, you took everything! You made yo point." Ant begged not even taking his face from the carpet which said to me he knew he was wasting his breath, but then again he can't take it with him.

"Yeah, I made my point to you Ant, and I doubt given the chance you'd play me like a fool again." I point the shotgun with Paul's prints on it at the back of Ant's head.

"But this a point I make for Paul's sake." I say before pulling the trigger leaving two holes in Ant's head.

CHAPTER 12

Mayor Church and two of his personal guards stand around a half-conscious Gage who was obviously beaten and drugged.

"So you say he said he work for Vegas?" The Mayor asks as he's looking through the same pictures that Gage sent Vegas. As the audio of the mayor and Junito end Junito walks into the warehouse.

"Yo creo que Conesco Suffiente de esta mujer Vegas. E yo Se de ariend que le encantra pnede La Mano a ese Conbarde entonce Alcadre Church yo te delo resorhe cone vejas ahora mismo. Per argien quiere hablar con ella horita." Junito says after the Mayor tells him who Gage is and what he was hired to do.

"Junito, like I said I'll take care of Vegas, but in no way am I asking you to kill this kid here. If we going to continue to do business I need to hear you say you have no plans to kill him." The Mayor stands toe to toe with Junito making sure his words are being heard.

"Mayor Church I hear you and understand you, I can give you my word but I can't say what Lorimar will do." Junito says in heavily-accented English with a smile on his face. "Lorimar doesn't want Vegas to know she's back in the States. If you're smart you wouldn't mention it either."

Still driving Gee's truck I was heading to my loft with the double barrel shotgun in my passenger seat. Killing Ant was necessary. It's times like this that I feel like Achilles from the movie Troy. I make kings, Ant forgot I made him. Maybe because I didn't come around enough to remind him, but hopefully Paul doesn't forget. My phone started to vibrate and I pick it up off the seat next to the shotgun. I see it's Gage and that reminds me how pissed he had me earlier.

"Nigga what the fuck is wrong with you!" I yell into the phone. I damn near crash when the voice I hear isn't Gage but the Mayor's.

"That's how you talk to an old friend Vegas?" The Mayor says. Clay got a way of sounding humorous-sarcastic, if that makes sense, you never know when he's serious and the few times I was around him I notice that he was good at disrespecting a person and the person never realized he had been disrespected.

This was too much for me to put together on the go like this so I pull over just a block from actually being downtown. An 'old friend' The Mayor and I were not. I went to High School at Cass Tech, me, Moose, and Ebony. The Mayor and Tots went to Renaissance where he was a star in baseball, he ended up playing triple A but he was never good enough to move up to the Major's. How he became Mayor last year is a mystery to me, how he got Gage's phone is a bigger one.

"Now Vegas, I want you to listen. I know from your friend Gage that you been following me, for who it doesn't matter, but I would like for us to meet p."

"Where's Gage?" I keep my question short not wanting to reveal how angry I am.

"He's right here, not in as good a condition as he was, but he'll live." I don't know if it's a good thing how calm and business-like Clay sounded or if it was reason for me to be worried for Gage.

"Can I see Gage just so I know what you telling me is true?"...

After I see Gage I know for sure I should be worried.

ALL GOOD A WEEK AGO

"Vegas, I'm the Mayor, I'm not a murderer. I promise I have no intentions of harming him." I wanted to yell and point out the fact that Gage was already harmed but I had to keep a clear head. Clay called me for a reason.

"So you want to meet. Where and will you bring Gage?" It's clear that I was out of my league if this was a nigga on the street I'll know just how to play this, but this was the fuckin' Mayor!

"1:00 AM meet me at the state fair grounds. Vegas, this is a meeting where a deal will be made. Not murder!" Clay ended the call never answering the question if Gage would be there. I can't see Clay killing him for some pictures and what, an audio… I start the truck and continue to my loft. I got about an hour and fifteen minutes to try and wrap my head around the fact that I may be the reason someone I love like a little brother is killed…

***

Now I'm in my Charger after taking a shower and changing into a black Nike sweat suit, I was still wearing my bulletproof vest. Clay might not be a murderer but I was and if I don't like what I see or hear… ain't no telling!

A meeting at this time of day, now I was in my comfort zone. With time to think I was prepared for anything even seeing Gage's dead body. I'll be lying if I was to say at first the thought wasn't painful, but there was only one way for Gage to have been caught that night. If the little nigga would've listened he wouldn't be sitting there now, not to say knowing this will affect how I handle this situation if Gage is hurt. Shi-it… I'll still go all out. At the end of the day I feel if you hurt somebody you know I care about you questioning my loyalty, you questioning my gun, and you questioning my reputation. So there's no reason that will make me not kill Clay tonight if he thinks he could get away with hurting Gage…

Usually the gate is locked to the State Fair grounds. With it getting close to summer I guess they were trying to keep it clean and secure. I see a weak security guard patrolling the area as I'm going deeper into the grounds approaching the only car here, must've pulled some strings being the Mayor and all.

I pull up to the driver side about ten feet away. I had no intentions of stepping out of the car until I saw something that made sense. At one in the morning there was a light chill and it wasn't too late that the City was asleep, but the feelings I was sensing wasn't welcoming.

Finally a big weight lifting nigga stepped from the passenger side. He looked more like the 'give a bullet' type than the 'take a bullet' type, so I was alert. I watch him go to the back door and open it. I thought the Mayor was getting out, instead the guy pulled out a duffle bag. Lost as I watched the big nigga put the duffle bag on the hood of my car thinking the whole time. What the fuck is in the bag! God only knows why I didn't pull off. Pulling out a phone he presses a number and knocks on my window.

"Window down," the nigga sounded like he had a tennis ball in his throat. Man this crazy! I let the window down just enough for him to slide the phone in. Instantly the man hopped back into the passenger seat of the black car then they pull off leaving me fucked up racking my brain about the possibilities of what was in that bag!

"What's in the duffle Clay?" I hope I sounded more stable than I felt because in my mind I was seeing Gage's head stuffed in that bag.

"Vegas, I need you to listen. Right now you stumbled on something bigger than the normal shit you deal with as a P.I."

"Nigga I said what's in the fuckin' bag!" I cut him off knowing I was sounding as tough and angry as I was feeling. The disrespect he just threw at me had me mad as hell, plus now I was thinking more crazy shit as I stepped out the car. It's crazy but Gage's head being in the bag was now the second worst thing that could be in the duffle bag on the hood of my car. I snatch one of my pistols out of its holster and walk about 30 feet away from my car.

"You're not in a position to demand answers Vegas, now we can do this my way or both you and your friend could be dead." Was he saying Gage was dead already or what? Rubbing my face

I take myself through my breathing... Calm down girly... Inhale... Exhale...

"So you ready to listen?"

"Yeah, I'm listening." It wasn't hard for me to humble myself, clearly Clay had me at a disadvantage.

"Smart." Clay chuckled, "now I know one of my opponents are paying you to catch me in some kind of scandal. Gage said you were hired to catch me cheating on my wife. Vegas, you stumbled on that and more." Clay stopped talking and I didn't know if he was looking for me to confirm that or what.

"So you not going to say yea or nay?" I take my time to gather my thoughts, he made this meeting so he already knows how he want this to end. In a case when dealing with information less is more.

"Yes Clay, I was hired to catch you cheating."

"Uh-huh, I have my sources, Vegas, so I think I know enough about you to know that the right amount of money can keep you from letting this out, yeah?"

"Clay, no amount of money will let me allow you to get away with killing Gage, understand!" I say this as calmly but firmly as I can as I stare at the duffle bag. I'm more than sure now that it was not a bomb in there. I can't think who Clay's sources may be and it didn't matter because they were wrong if they think the worst thing that can happen is me letting this out if Gage is killed.

"Let's stick to your case, then we can talk about the killing of Gage. Can he be trusted? Who knows... I'm going to put it plain to you Vegas because we at the point where choices must be made. In that duffle bag is two hundred grand. We not going to act like we both don't know who the other holds dearly to their heart." Clay didn't have to say more for me to get the threat. In Detroit we had Mayors in our history to be found doing dirty shit. I believe Clay was telling me that he's willing to pay to keep this deal from getting out and he was also wiling to kill if it does get out.

"What about Gage? Where is he?" This was going to decide everything. It's the people that I love that I was putting in harm's way if I decided not to play ball with Clay. I know this but if he did wrong by Gage I really felt I had no choice...

"Tell me you accepting the money for your silence and I wouldn't mind if you stayed on the case a little while longer Vegas... So we have a deal?"

This contract must be something bigger than I think. I can't see why I can't accept this deal. Shid... if Gage was dead I wasn't planning on exposing Clay, I was planning on killing him.

"I don't know why, but I trust you Vegas." Hearing Clay sound so cheerful pissed me off! "Now to your friend Gage... Well it seems you have bigger problems than me. I..." I cut Clay off!

"What the fuck you mean Clay!!!" I scream into the phone.

"As you know I have a partner, you have audio of us talking. Well he took Gage. Before you cut me off again, he promised he wasn't going to kill him, but he said somebody else wanted to see him. Something about her having unfinished business with you. I don't know who she is and whatever that means. Before today I never knew you two knew each other." Now Clay was really talking as if we were old friends.

"Clay I don't know who that man is, I never met him before and who is the 'she' he's talking about?" I was no longer pissed but I was now very worried about Gage. I don't have too many 'she' enemies, but the ones I do are dangerous.

"Well that's the thing, I don't know her Vegas. Just that she didn't want you to know she was back in the state but," I end the call with Clay. There was nothing more he could tell me. Unknown to him maybe, but if he know it or not Gage's life was still tied to his. I take the duffle bag off my hood and throw it in the passenger seat as I start my Charger, I had a lot to think about.

CHAPTER 13

This Sunday morning was not one of my best. I got to my loft at 2:30AM and ended up oversleeping until 6:30AM. Needing some exercise I got Tricks and hit Detroit Mercy's outside track. I was far from myself as I sit in my Charger in front of the Holy Water, now at 9AM my mind still wasn't clear. I was trying hard to come up with a plan to find out who got Gage and get him back alive. With so much going on I couldn't give all my attention to that. I wish I could sit here and enjoy thinking about what I'm going to do with that two hundred thou that I had at my loft. I hit many licks and this was the easiest two hundred thousand I ever got. Had me thinking I been taking advantage of the wrong people. Even so I knew people like Clay was playing by a different set of rules than I been playing by.

I could've sat there for hours and never come up with a name of anybody in the streets who'd snatch up Gage. Clay's people did it without a second thought. I had to put this to the side for now even though Quan was back at the top of my list of things to do.

Could Flex be the woman Clay was speaking of? It's hard for me to see Flex as female, but until I cross him out I couldn't say for sure that Flex wasn't the person who's holding Gage hostage. I really couldn't see Clay, Junito, and Quan having any business connections. There was a woman I had in mind but I was not ready to think, nor could I afford to give the necessary energy I'll need to get her. Not until Quan was completely out the picture then I'll turn my attention to her and I need to be stronger with my thoughts to stop them from returning to that problem.

Seeing a white Porsche truck pull up behind me instantly shut down thoughts of Quan. I knew it was Rich Tony because he's the only nigga I fuck with in the City with a white Porsche truck. After what I did at his blood house I wasn't surprised to see the sour look on his face. Rich Tony's fat ass hopped out dressed in his usual Gucci sweat suit. I unlock my doors and turn down the music.

"Big boy, what up doh!" I ask Rich Tony once he's situated in the passenger seat.

"Shit, I just got back into the City… Muthafuckas was hitting me up crazy about one of my houses burning down. I see yo shit got firebombed too. So what you think?" Since Rich Tony put it like that I could see why he would be asking me about things.

"I wasn't hip to yo shit going up in flames but this shit right here… This shit here is personal. It wasn't connected to yo shit." Now that I think about it I really don't know who did this shit to Rev's bar. I just assumed it was Quan but now! Man this shit was probably bigger than the little shit I had going on with Quan.

"Ri-ight." Rich Tony says this as he looks my way. "I'm just coming from the police station. They say they found a body in the ashes."

"Yeah?" I say this nonchalantly… "So what, you want to hire me or something?" Rich Tony was throwing me off. I don't see why he was here talking to me about his shit.

"Naw, I don't have nosey neighbors and they used to seeing people going in and out of there, so when the boys asked did they see something strange they said nah. But one of my people told me he seen three females coming from there and two had 'Police' across their hats." Rich Tony was looking out the window as he spoke. Thus was one of them times when information was best kept to yourself until it was useful, unless Rich Tony was planning on extorting me him hipping me to this was confusing. I wasn't trying to set Rich Tony up by leaving that body in his shit, in fact I wasn't thinking about him at all. I just needed an empty house. Police finding a body in his shit and now he's here talking to me, now that was something I'll have to think about when I got time.

"Okay and?" With all that's going on I couldn't let Rich Tony think for a minute he had something on me. Other than that I couldn't care less about him thinking he had something on me, he and I both know I'll fuck his whole life up! So when he turned and smiled it really pissed me off.

"I just thought that little information would be something you'll want to know."

"Right now I can't see that info being useful, but thanks." Hopefully Rich Tony could hear and see the irritation and drop the subject.

"Cool. So when the spot opening back up?"

"Shid... I don't know. Rev left it up to me to get shit fixed, they'll be starting tomorrow. Just to fuck wit him I'm thinking of changing a thing or two around." Rich Tony chuckled. Knowing me he knew there was a chance I would. Rich Tony stayed and we chopped it up for a while as we smoked some shit he brought from Canada.

I did nothing the whole day, which is a rare occasion for me. I didn't make no money, I didn't get no pussy, or get in a shout out, but it was only eight so it was still early. I'm at my loft now on the internet buying furniture like a housewife; wasn't getting in a shoot out, pussy, or getting no money doing this. But what really could I do? I still had a couple of my contacts on the lookout for Quan but I wasn't going to go out there and start looking under rocks for him. The best news came in today when Short Fuse hit me up to tell me the ticket was off my head. I guess Quan a.k.a.

Flex finally strapped his nuts on and decided to try his hand. Three bodies in less than a week, niggas probably wasn't lining up to come at me no more anyways. Knowing this did have me feeling safe, but right now both cases was out of my hands. I didn't like having nothing to do so when Moose called and told me about Jssiah's concert I wasn't sure I'd go, but now I was leaning toward going. Tots took my advice and went down to Dallas now instead of later, that was a good thing, but I really had nothing to do… I guess I could call up Sara or Brittany but my mind wasn't in it. Now Ebony! That's something I'm gonna think about…

A concert on a Sunday! Only Jssiah would think this was a good idea, he was taking this Prophet shit too far. Since Spokes was a big fan of Jssiah, and I know he's only 13, but I still told him to get dressed and hop on his new GSX-R 1000 bike and meet me in front of COBO. I'm not gonna lie, thinking of Gage played a big part in my decision to bring Spokes to the concert. For years I been putting them both in danger even though I love and look at them both as little brothers I see that I didn't really treat them as such. Giving them money and really overpaying them, the streets will have you thinking that was enough and alright, like money justified everything. Really where would either of them be without me? With no family Gage I doubt would be in college right now. Spokes you might as well say he has no family either. I got him his own studio apartment and a garage for his bikes and shit. Yeah, they would've had nothing without me but with little problems I could've put them in better positions and used them differently. I was late to these thoughts. Hopefully in the future I will be better to both if given the chance. No matter how much I'd like to believe that there was a good chance that Quan a.k.a. Flex was involved with Gage being held hostage really I knew he wasn't. If Gage was to make it out of this alive, and that was a small chance if it's who I think is involved in this, he would never be the same again. This I knew from experience!

Stepping out of my shower I grab a towel and dry off in front of my floor to ceiling mirror, knowing deep down that Lorimar had Gage. It only made sense. If Junito wasn't Spanish then maybe I wouldn't be so sure. Getting Quan out of the way was something I needed to do with the quickness, Lorimar and her family weren't nothing to fuck with halfway! Looking at my face was all the reminder I needed although it wasn't her but her brother who ordered my face to be plunged into the aquarium that was filled with piranhas. Lorimar for sure was responsible for me being in that position. I look at my scars and I find myself with that same smirk as always. If Lorimar is the woman holding Gage I was more than glad to get some pay back... I blow a kiss at my reflection and shake my head knowing that following this line of thought could get real dark quick.

 I was dressed in a pair of tight short shorts with the white Louis Vuitton suspenders to match my Louis Vuitton sports bra and knee high stockings I was Louis Vuitton down to the shoes.

 Even though me and Jssiah was cool and Moose was family I knew they wasn't letting me in the concert with my pistols V.I.P. passes or not. But I was hoping that I could slide in with my knife strapped. Spokes walked in with me through the V.I.P. back entrance. He was looking young as ever, fresh though in an Off White outfit more like a uniform but the little nigga knew how to wear his clothes I'll give him that with his little iced out Cartier watch. The most important thing Spokes had on him was his fake I.D. Instead of money Spokes requested the I.D. for his first payment, ending up costing him his first three jobs! You know I had to get him. Looking at the I.D. I had to smile. It was top notch, but I didn't have to overcharge the little nigga...

 I have to give credit to Jssiah. His concerts were unique. The first thing you notice is that Jssiah's stage is not 8 feet to 12 feet high, so you're not looking up at him or so far away you gotta see him on screen. That's probably because we were in COBO and not a stadium but Jssiah believing he is who he is I think even in a stadium he'd make sure his fans was as close as he could get them and the scene as intimate as it is now. Instead Jssiah's stage was more like 5 feet high and I don't know how many feet wide, it was very spacious. Instead of a back stage or a room where other artists might stay Jssiah was sitting on stage watching the local rappers he picked up to open up for him. There wasn't a crowd standing or sitting in front of the stage either. You can come and stand inches from the stage. Jssiah had it set up to where it was like twenty if not more stations spread out around the stage with wrap around couches, tables, and chairs. Each station held about 20 people comfortably. It was a laid back vibe with bars spread out also.

By the time me and Spokes got in through the back Jssiah was between sets, letting an instrumental play as he sparked up a blunt sitting on a couch to the side where every section can see him. Jssiah was talking and vibing with his fans, talking shit, sharing his mind. He was versatile so his music was attractive to most of the City. I was seeing all the big boys and females in his V.I.P. section on stage, a stick up kid heaven I wouldn't be surprised if a couple niggas become victims ta'night. If I knew Jssiah, and I do, he'll have his East Warren niggas following somebody...

Jssiah was sitting with some of the groupies, big time rappers, and dope boys of the City when he saw me. Like most times he greeted me like childhood friends which caused me to get a lot more attention from the others than I wanted since my intentions were to come out and chill hoping to duck off. I mean it wasn't like there were many niggas up here I didn't know and I doubt if they didn't know me or at least heard of me, so it was more stares than words exchanged. I was glad Spokes decided to find somewhere else to duck off to, wouldn't want one of these niggas to associate him with me, I'd hate for another Gage situation. Although I like to believe none of these niggas was stupid enough to try me like that but Rev taught me a long time ago never believe you know what a person will or won't do.

Knowing Moose was on duty I went looking for her in the wrong places but as I move deeper into the stage area, away from the front, I see Moose with two females cozy up on a couch. I should've known!

"What up doh cuz!" Moose says once she take her lips from the ear of a bad bitch and realize I was standing in front of her table which like every table I had seen so far was covered with drugs and alcohol. Moose's drip was crazy too, in Amirie and red bottoms. She had diamonds everywhere looking like a rapper/dope boy, she wasn't here to do no security. She made me want to hide my little bust down AP! After seeing Moose I was more comfortable and relaxed so I gave Moose a smile and a nod as I picked up the bottle of D'usse. Leaving Moose to her friends I went to find me a spot to chill and try to enjoy Jssiah's show.

30 minutes in and I had me a nice amount of D'usse in me. I been smoking some of that shit from Canada Rich Tony left me with as well. I was feeling good, Jssiah was just ending another song when I stood up, lighting another blunt I went looking for Spokes. Taking the way back down the stage I see Moose and her two baddies were getting touchy-feely, a nice amount of drugs and alcohol was gone. Moose didn't do hard drugs so I wasn't worried about her but she knew how to get a bitch loose.

Times like this were the only times I wish I had a dick, because unless I put on a skirt, which I'm not gonna do, but if I did other than that I gotta do too much to get a quick nut! Niggas just pull they shit out anytime and anywhere and go to work. Shit ain't right! I was very surprised to see Slick here. He and Eastside Rick were surrounded by white hoes. Walking past them I raise my bottle and like at Slick's crib my eyes met the chick with the dreads, I have to holla at Slick and get the ticket on that. I notice there were more people moving around mingling. Jssiah concerts always feel like a social gathering. There weren't too many dark areas one could duck off to. It was very open, but the third section from the end I was coming from was dark and smaller than the others which made it stand out. I see someone knocked the light out and sectioned off the opening. It wasn't hard to figure out what was going on. Jssiah was back on stage, he was performing one of his laid back songs and I was close enough to hear what was going on; whoever was back there was giving some super wet head. I was going to keep walking but I hear Spokes' voice and he was loving it! Never been one to hate so I posted up and vibed out to Jssiah thinking it was gonna be quick, but it turned out he was just starting. Spokes was in rare form. He had me thinking of the time I got Gage his first pussy…

By the time Jssiah finished with his song the female was coming out of the self-made fort, had me thinking she was one of Jssiah's self-promoted hoes… in fact I was sure she was. She was nice thick redbone. Bitch was a real pro the way she put herself back together like that. Would've never known she was just fuckin' by looking at her now. Still in the cut I waited on Spokes who finally came out smiling as he lit a blunt.

"Little nigga I see you." I say smiling as Spokes jump and look my way. I was lit from drinking this D'usse from the neck and that shit from Canada had me floating. Spokes didn't say shit. He was just smiling as I put my arm around his shoulder and led him toward the stage. A few times he reached for the D'usse, but I wasn't that lit.

"Spokes, you know you turned that chick into a child molester right?" I chuckle thinking if she seen him in the light. The nigga was 13 but he could pass for 16 at the most, because of his height, but he looked young. But then again I knew his age so that may have played a part on why he didn't look older to me.

"Hell nah! That was Melody, bitch only 16. I was in middle school with her." I had to stop and laugh, this shit was crazy!

Jssiah was back on the stage and I was looking for somewhere to sit. The drink and weed was getting to me and I was hoping this was the last song. I was ready to go but I wasn't leaving Spokes and it seemed like he just got here the way he was acting plus I promised I'd introduce him to Jssiah, shit the little nigga knew every song. He was a real fan! Looking around I see the last thing I expected to see, and it knocked the D'usse and weed right outta me. Sitting with two dyke bitches was Quan, a.k.a. Flex and he was definitely Flex ta'night as he sat between the two studs. I wasn't too drunk or mad not to think. I made sure I was blocking Quan from seeing Spokes if he was to look this way.

I bump Spokes to get his attention.

"Spokes... Spokes!" While elbowing him I say his name, little nigga was too caught up in the song so I had to turn to him so he could see my face.

"Spokes! Look behind me!" I move to the side slightly.

"See that tranny in the white?"

"Yeah, I can't see his face like that but I know who you talking about."

"Right. I want you to go outside and once you see him leave I want you to follow him."

"WHAT?!? Jssiah ain't done! That nigga can take forever to leave... Come on Vegas!" I wasn't really paying attention to Spokes' every word, I was too busy peeking over my shoulder toward Quan.

"Listen Spokes, he'll be coming outta here soon trust me. Now go!" I didn't even wait to make sure Spokes did as I said before I was taking my AP off and stuffing it in my pocket making sure the top was tight on my bottle in case I have to use it. I told Spokes this bitch nigga was coming out, that was only because I didn't have my babies with me.

Quan was wearing all white Chanel from the floor up. I was having visions of turning that shit red! Ugly nigga was taking it too far with that lace front on. In any other scenario seeing him in that wig would've made me laugh but now it only made me madder. By the time I got to Quan's section he was just looking up from snorting a line, of what I don't know. I didn't have to be a genius when I looked around to know that this possibly could end bad for me. There were about 30 people in his section and I wasn't counting on getting no help if this nigga was to get on my ass. But I was too charged up to think about that.

I charged into his section making sure I keep the bottle down, I didn't want to give any indication whether I was going to throw it or if I was hoping to get close enough to swing it. I was about two feet away from the table when Quan and both dykes with him jumped up. With the bottle in my right hand I threw it across my body aiming for the dyke on my left catching her in the face. Instantly chaos erupted! I wasn't paying much attention to anyone or anything but the nigga in front of me, but I was happy to see the other dyke go to her friend instead of helping Quan deal with me. It seemed to me like more noise than movement was going on before I knew it I was I being pushed by Quan and I was flying!

The nigga was strong! You know how some gay niggas become completely bitches in every way like they were never men, well Quan wasn't like that! I got up and came at him again. Nothing was in our way and it didn't seem like anybody was planning to jump in. How someone can look at this scene and not think something was wrong is crazy…

Quan wasn't fucking around. His reach was longer than mine so when he reached out and smacked me it shocked me cause I thought I wasn't close at all. The smack drew blood from my lip and seeing the smirk on his face I knew what he was thinking as he smacked me again, but this time I didn't let it faze me I kept taking small steps towards him.

"Bitch, I can do this all night!" Quan said in his man voice smiling as he takes another swing at my face which I block. Now I had my fist up looking like a female Iron Mike stalking him.

"Okay Vegas, you wanna box? Now y'all see this…" The nigga act like he didn't just smack me twice. He was still talking when I cut him off with a straight jab to his mouth.

It had less effect than I would have liked because when I tried to follow it with another quick jab Quan pushed me with all his might causing me to stumble and trip. I quickly hopped up and backed out of Quan's section. He didn't stop but instead kept following me with pure hatred in his eyes as we squared up.

"I been waiting for this for years!" Quan growled. I doubt if anybody but me could hear him. Quan attacked me but not as wild as I would've hoped. With one step he closed the gap enough to fake jab with his right and hit me with a nice left. It would've put me down I'm sure if I wasn't quick with my block. My forearm was in major pain. Like I said, this nigga was strong. I countered with a nice body shot and I heard the breath leave him, but it wasn't enough. When I went for a hook Quan blocked it and hit me with one of his own dropping me to one knee... Blood was leaking from my eye like crazy. I was just wiping it from my face when Quan started coming toward me. I was breathing hard and in pain. I charged Quan with a desperate goal to scoop him. Bad idea! Like I said before the nigga had thighs like a running back. He stumbled back and I was still hugging his waist when he literally planted his feet and all movement stopped. I was in a bad position and I knew it was over. Quan hit me so hard in my ribs I thought he broke three at least.

"AHHH!" I screamed and those were the first words I spoke since making the big mistake of coming into his section. If Quan proved one thing tonight it was that he still had some nigga in him and I was for sure going to remember that.

"OH SHIT! Is that Vegas I see getting it in? I got 5 bands on my dawg!" I hear Jssiah on the mic. This nigga must be seeing the wrong fight. Shid, I'll take that bet and I had no intentions of throwing the fight!

After the body shot Quan swung me from around his waist and I ended up landing on the same ribs he just hit me in. Damn I was in crazy pain and was really considering running but Quan wasted no time. He surprised me with how quickly he pounced on me trying to put me in a choke hold. I did everything I could to keep my arm up between his arm and my throat but I knew it was only a matter of time until he'll have me in a sleeper. I just didn't have the strength to last much longer. I would just have to let him get his choke and use my last energy fighting...

I was now clawing, elbowing, and kicking. This sick nigga was licking and nibbling on my ear while talking shit to me.

"Vegas, don't pass out... because if you do I'm gonna drag you outta here, take you back to my spot and rape you, I promise." Quan said this in his sickest voice as he grind against my ass making sure I felt his dick getting hard. No doubt about it I believed him but what could I do, I was starting to see spots and wishing I had my pistols.

I was in fanatic mode trying to save what little breath I had as I slapped and clawed at Quan's arms. It was no use... this nigga had that crazy strength, I was sure of it now. My hand slipped off of Quan's arm and that's when my hand brushed against my knife handle... Saved my life, because I was done for! I didn't have time to think I just snatched my knife out and blindly started stabbing at Quan's arm. Now it was clear to me why multiple stab wounds is an indication of a crime of passion, you had to really hate a person to continue to stab them over and over; withdraw, stab, withdraw and stab. I was feeling my knife going into Quan's arm and the path it traveled before nicking his bone every time. I was loving it! It was on my third stab that Quan had had enough and with a loud yell Quan released my neck and unluckily rolled right into a perfect soccer style kick from Moose red bottom to the face! I just took in one huge breath to fill my lungs. My adrenaline was up and I was drunk from the sensation of those first three stabs. I hop up with my bloody knife. There was chaos all around me, but my eyes were on Quan who was just now getting up holding his face. Blood was leaking from the small holes left by Moose's red bottom spikes. Quan's arm was a mess and I could still see the crazy in his eyes, only now he was looking like a person who just woke up in hell and didn't remember how he got there. His movements said that he was in panic mode as he looked around, for what I don't know. Behind him I saw Moose throwing hands with one of the dykes. Quan was stumbling past her when one of his homies grabbed his arm and pulled him. I was moving as fast as I could, no matter what though I couldn't get enough air in my lungs and my throat was killing me every time I yelled or swallowed. Clearly I wasn't moving fast at all I was just passing Moose and I barely could see Quan who was still being pulled toward an exit, that's when I heard somebody scream, "GUN!"

    Hearing that stopped me. I dove for the nearest cover which was a bar thinking 'why didn't I bring my guns?' Lord knows I should've tried! Really Moose and Jssiah couldn't stop me...

    I peek around the bar and I wasn't seeing shit but legs. Getting off my knees I continue to look around. Gazing to where I saw Moose last she was standing over some nigga with her gun aimed at him. It looked like she was saying something and she kept touching her face bringing her fingers back bloody every time. Moose kicked the shit out of the nigga before shooting him twice in the leg or ass, I couldn't tell exactly where.

Now knowing it was only Moose with a gun I get up and head her way dodging people. Out of irritation I stuck my foot out to trip a person or two. I'm not going to lie, my body was aching and I don't know what Moose was thinking shooting somebody in these surroundings. I yell her name. It took a few times but when she turned around I saw her face was fucked up. It looked like her nose was broken and she had blood coming from the corners of her eyes.

"What up, Cuz?" Moose sounded calm but she was breathing hard and I was sure her nose was broken by the sound her breathing made. After addressing me she kicked the nigga in the back of the head since he was lying face down clearly in pain from the two bullets.

"This bitch nigga snuck me and did me bad!" Moose said, spitting on the nigga. Looking at her I wanted to get a couple kicks in, but I knew to anybody looking this shit would seem crazy, especially once they find out Moose is a cop.

"Moose you staying. Cops gonna be here, I'm trying to get outta here fast!" This shit was over and getting questioned ta'night was a hard no!

"Shit Cuz, I'mma stay. I'mma have to deal with this shit anyways." Being a cop she really couldn't escape this shit. I doubt if she was thinking clearly when she put two in that nigga. Unlike me, Moose liked being a cop and I knew for a fact this wasn't going to end well for her, but what the fuck? I had my hands full so I couldn't help. This nigga Quan had to be dealt with.

CHAPTER 14

"Damn!" I moan as I move, my body was a mess. My stitches were open and my neck had a crazy bruise around it from that choke hold Quan had me in. Every breath I took hurt like hell. Sara brought me a mirror, I also had a nice black eye. That shit at COBO made the news, knowing I was there you wouldn't be jumping off a cliff to think it had something to do with me, not if you knew me at all.

So Sara came to check on me. She was here 30 minutes after I got to my loft. With no furniture I was still lying on my floor going through my phone seeing if Spokes hit me up when she got here. With her help I made it to my bathroom where she ran water for me then washed me. I wasn't that fucked up but she seemed to be concerned so I let her play the part.

It was just 5am and I hadn't been asleep yet. My mind been going in circles. Spokes still hadn't hit me up or answered the phone. There was no telling, I couldn't put him in the same position I put Gage in, and this will be my fault for sure. I haven't even told anybody about Gage. Outside of the obvious people, Gage and Spokes are my family, my little brothers. And Gage I know is in big danger if Lorimar got his ass. But there was no need for me to get emotional about Spokes, I still had a chance it's not even for sure he's in any danger, I was letting my mind run wild and letting my fears take over my thinking. Before Emilio I was never like this!

With everything going down last night Spokes probably just needed some sleep. Speaking of sleep I wonder how Sara could sleep with me resting between her legs with my head on her stomach. Crazy, shit had to be a little uncomfortable for her. I'm far from being ready for a serious relationship and Sara seems to be cool with that but she slowly been coming around more and she introduced me to her brother Sam. We have done business since then on some guns and she talked to me about the rest of her family and their dislike of her choice of sexual partners, them being Muslim and all…

Man all this going on and here I'm thinking about this shit! Quan had me in a position I never been in before, never have I had this hard of a time killing a nigga. I had nothing on Quan. I couldn't find him and nobody so far had a line on him. I fucked up, I should've set on Ant and waited for him and Quan to link up, but I was in my bag. Quan hasn't been around or hit Paul up, it didn't matter though. How Quan's story was going to end was already written, I'm just waiting for him so I could put the last period down.

Normally, for no other reason but it being Monday, me waking up and reaching for my gun would've made sense. But today I was woken by a shock from my subconscious a couple hours into my sleep. Rev and Joyce were the reason today. Happy that Sara was already up and gone my Monday morning alarm clock was unknown to all. Pain shooting through my body put me back down instantly. I was breathing hard but I was up and could tell already that I was going to have to take it slow today. On my back looking up at the ceiling I was racking my brain. What, Rev and Joyce been gone two… three days? Shit been so crazy I can't say for sure and I don't remember if I heard from them since they've been gone.

Somehow my phone was under me and it took all my power not to scream from the pain coming from my bruised if not broken ribs. Looking at their social media it wasn't a real surprise that they hadn't posted in days. Rev and Joyce are both old school, they also haven't called or left a message for me, that was 50/50 cause to worry. So I decided to call Rev.

He didn't answer so I left a message telling him to get back to me ASAP! I tried to make it sound as urgent as possible. I wasn't in panic mode but I was worried and when I called Joyce and didn't get an answer it was more alarming because she always answers. This wasn't a good thing and I could be overreacting or overthinking this, I was going off a subconscious shake. But with Lorimar, Emilio, or any part of their family on the prowl there was no such thing as overreacting or thinking, you could never be too careful. I felt the worst is always possible...

I called Tots just to make sure she was safe at mom's and I put her in the loop with what had me spooked leaving out Lorimar since I still hadn't told her about Gage. I was hoping still to right that wrong. Her social was buzzing about the shit at COBO last night so I ran her through that.

Before getting in the tub and soaking I called Spokes and left another message once he didn't answer. I was wrapping an Ace bandage around my ribs when Spokes finally hit me back.

"Vegas, my bad! But I couldn't call or answer you. I was in the house with them niggas..." I cut Spokes off, he sounded excited and outta breath.

"What! They caught you?" I had nothing to worry about, clearly I was back to jumping to the worst possible situation. Spokes told me after following them from COBO to a house he waited and snuck in through a basement window. A while back I remember asking Spokes how he always found his way into people's shit.

He told me that when he was younger, the nigga was 13 so I don't know how much younger he could've been, but anyways his mom had them living in a shelter. So after school most days he'll go to a friend's house and chill and once it got time to leave he'll leave like he was going home and double back and sneak into their crib and find some place to sleep either in the basement or if they had one, the attic. Spokes said he just got good at opening windows or breaking into them with little or no sound, after hearing this that's when I grabbed him that one room studio apartment. I'm sure with the money I pay him he looks out for his sibling who live with other family members. The little nigga was only 13 but on these streets nobody really pays attention or cares, if you playing out here, then you out here. No matter what I thought now I know I'm getting soft, but Spokes would be worse off without me.

"Okay, after you followed and snuck in what happened?" Knowing he was alright I was back to the important shit and that's trying to find a way to Quan.

"Shit Vegas the she/he nigga called some hood doctor over and got cleaned up. But Vegas, that he/she nigga is crazy man! I don't know if the nigga hate or love you the way he was talking," I didn't need or want to hear what Spokes meant about that.

"Yeah, I know Spokes, but tell me did you see Cherry?"

"You talking about my African Queen Cherry?!? She fuckin' wit them?" I forgot this nigga was infatuated with that bitch and I don't know what made me ask about her anyways!

"Little nigga calm down, but yeah, her." I could hear Spokes taking deep breaths.

"Nah Vegas, nobody was in there and I was all in they shit. I think that's just a spot they chill at. Wasn't even no furniture in there." Hearing that had me looking around.

"It started getting wild in there after the doc left. Man I just got outta there!" Wild could've meant anything but Spokes has me thinking some freaky shit was going on.

"Alright Spokes, what street they on?"

"Lindsay off Joy road." Damn that's right there. Quan was playing a dangerous game. It's crazy the nigga bought some titties and some nuts! We talked for a while more about nothing.

"Okay little nigga, get some sleep. I'll talk to you later."

It was 10:00am now and I had to be at the Holy Water by 10:45. I still couldn't get ahold of Rev or Joyce but I couldn't do anything about that. I popped two pain pills and downed two Red Bulls taking the rest of the 6-pack with me out the front door.

It was a sunny day and that just added to my misery. With my ribs bandaged up I needed to be in something loose. I was dressed in hoop gear plus I had my bulletproof vest on, sunglasses, and a fitted.

I was in my Charger watching the clean up crew pull out the damaged interior of the Holy Water, it was worse than I thought a couple days ago and to find out the fire did reach Rev's apartment, nothing major but it reached it! With Quan so close it took everything in me not to drive over there and put 30 in his head, why I didn't I don't know. Stop it! Who was I kidding? My body wasn't up for it but I was putting something together in my head as I watch praying these guys hurry up.

Seven's gold Navigator crept past before finding a parking spot. With this crew and this big-ass garbage can in front of the Holy Water Seven had to park a block away and walk back. 'I can just imagine what this nigga want,' I think as I unlock my door and let Seven's big ass get comfortable. Nigga looked like the Hulk in my shit, I didn't like that shit at all!

"Damn boss lady, you look like something." Seven has a way of sounding stupid and he do it in a way that makes you think he's doing it on purpose, but I knew better. Plus the nigga had a fat kid jolliness to him that's hard not to laugh when he looks at you and his chubby face breaks into a smile. That's what he was trying to do now, but you could tell he had something serious on his mind, so I took it easy on him and smiled back hoping it would speed him up and get to his reason for being here.

"So what up, fat boy?"

"Shit, just checking on you and the place." Seven says as he looks through the window toward The Holy Water. I see I was going to have to help the fool.

"Nigga yeah right! You came through because Brittany told yo silly ass I'll find Cherry." I chuckle when he turns around and raises them thick stupid-ass eyebrows. This light skin nigga was the last nigga in the City with a S-Curl.

"How you know?" We both burst out laughing. "But Vegas, you find anything?" The big nigga softened up real quick! Damn this nigga was in love with Cherry I see.

"Man, I think I know where she's at, and she still in the City I think."

"Shid, let's go! We don't need nobody! Just you and me." The nigga was smiling and talking fast.

"Seven calm down, I said 'I think,' let me find out for sure."

"What she in danger you think?" I know he thinks he sounded and looked tough but I never seen a nigga so big look so small as he did now worried about Cherry.

"Yeah, if she's where I think she is th-" Seven cut me off.

"Well let's go Vegas! Come on! You know me, come on you know... Man I'm just sayin... Man we was talking about getting married and shit..." Seven looked at me and pulled out an engagement ring and I could see tears in his eyes. I know when a nigga just want to vent so I just sat back not saying a word; I just let the nigga go.

"Vegas she told me about the nigga Quan and what you did for her. I talked to her mom and shit, you know everybody's worried about her." Seven pulled out a big-ass four-five.

"Vegas no bullshit when you go get her I'm trying to be a part of it. Please... That nigga got my wife."

Shit I don't know how he knew about Quan having Cherry but shit, who was I to stop a nigga from saving his wife. Anyways, I only cared about killing Quan, I'd let Seven play the prince... I was looking over to Seven and thinking how I could use him, a plan started to form.

It was around 6:00pm and I was starving sitting in the corned beef shop waiting on Spokes, at least I left a message for him to meet me here, little nigga was back to not answering the phone. My phone was vibrating as I was telling the waitress to bring me a corned beef cut in half with extra cheese and two pickles. I was starting on my second six pack and sixth pain pill.

"Whatupdo, Mo!" I answer after downing a Red Bull.

"Shit cuz, just left the station." Moose was sounding sober, not her usual self at all.

"Muthafuckas just suspended me and now I got that bitch nigga from Internal Affairs on my line again!" Damn I knew she was going to be in some shit and with that fuck nigga on her heels it was going to get worse. I was feeling for her, but I had my own shit going on so I couldn't give her too much of my attention or energy.

"You'll be cool cuz, fuck it!" I put more juice in those words than I felt. (Ay, I'm trying...)

"Cuz, I'm cool… Jssiah asked me to play security for him on this mini tour, what you think?" Man, what did I think? Maybe I'm giving myself more credit than I should but the first thing I was thinking was this nigga coming for me too! Because I can't see how these two muthafuckas got so close. But after thinking about it they do kind of fit together, I know Moose don't want nothing but some groupie love.

"Nigga do you. Might as well take a little vacation, but watch that nigga and know he is moving drugs. Jssiah is gonna test you so stay on yo P's and Q's." At the end of the day Jssiah knew she was family so she really had nothing to worry about, but then again you never really know.

"Cuz you sure? I know you got that shit with Quan." Moose wasn't just saying that she was for sure cocked and ready anytime I need her and if Seven wasn't prepared to follow me blindly I'd ask her to roll out with me.

"Moose that shit gonna be over with soon. I'm done playing around with that nigga." My tone said enough and Moose knew that topic was over.

Lindsay was a small street off Livernois. I wanted to have Spokes here earlier to make sure Quan was in there but the little nigga still wasn't answering his phone. If I didn't have Seven with me and his 'Captain save a hoe' intentions I would've just had four niggas here with AR's and that would be that. Instead I couldn't get in contact with Spokes and I did have Seven with me, so the plan was different.

Parked a couple blocks from Lindsay at an old school I had Seven and two of his boys meet me here. I knew I was pushing it, being in Gee's truck, but fuck it! I was already being reckless by having Seven and his boys with me, but if Seven was looking to get Cherry back that was him and his boys' job. I didn't know how many niggas Quan had with him. Hopefully Seven and them could handle them long enough for me to kill Quan, plus if things went as I planned, shid… I rather kill Seven and his homies than niggas I fuck with… Come on, you know I just can't have random niggas walking around after seeing me kill somebody, that's ammunition I can't allow a nigga to have against me.

After making sure everybody understood that this wasn't a shoot first situation and that this was a simple kick in the door job. I was trying to catch Quan off guard with only a few niggas with him. The last thing we want is bullets flying and niggas running. Seven and his boys came together in a Ram truck. The plan was to leave the trucks at the middle school and walk the few blocks to Lindsay. It wasn't late, only around 9:00pm on a Monday, so there were people about but this area wasn't too crowded. Since we were coming from the school we were behind the house Quan was in. Seven and Mike took the alley. Me and Fish took the front way and walked up the block. Fish's name fit him well and when Seven introduced us I broke out laughing, so did Seven and Mike. The nigga Fish had some big dumb-ass eyeballs and he looked exactly like a fish in a fish bowl. No bullshit the nigga couldn't hit a lick in the daytime without sunglasses or a mask, ain't no way! But he was one of them ugly niggas who had jokes so he went hard on Seven.

I didn't have my shoulder holster on, instead I had my pistol in my waistband, and I still had my vest under my jersey. With my adrenaline up I wasn't feeling any pain.

Walking up the stairs I uncover my pistol butt, I had to reach out a hand to stop Fish from knocking on the door and then I checked the door to see if it was unlocked, and it was! I learned a while ago that street niggas rarely lock their doors. I tell Fish to go get Seven and hurry up. I was thinking 'before he do something stupid,' but I didn't say it. Fish probably knew I was saying it in my head.

Once again I made sure everybody understood what the plan was. From the outside you could tell that the living room was to our right. I remind them to make as little noise as possible. I let Seven take the lead and moved to the back and we went in quickly.

Just as Spokes said there wasn't a piece of furniture anywhere. There was trash everywhere and the house smelled stale like it's been abandoned but the paint and the floors said otherwise. Bottles, blunt roaches, and cigarette butts covered the floor like ashtrays weren't invented yet. But what was drawing all our attention was the fat-ass nigga who was snoring loudly in the middle of the floor with a Draco across his belly. Quietly we all surround him trying to avoid the fast-food wrappers. All of us had our guns pointing at him before I could even demonstrate to Mike how to snatch the Draco. Mike was quick with snatching the gun off the nigga's belly and Seven's big ass jumped on the nigga putting him in a choke hold similar to the one Quan had me in. As Seven struggled with him I waited till I got the perfect shot and kicked the nigga in the nuts bringing all his struggling to an end. He let out a whine-like yell that caused the rest of us to step back and look toward the entrance to the living room. Moving that way, clearly it was time for us to search the rest of the house, so Mike and I left Seven and Fish.

Shit wasn't going to be that easy. I was pissed when I came back from checking the rest of the house. The same scene in the living room was in the other rooms. They were just as empty. I was fully prepared to end Quan's life right here, knowing that I was still far from bringing this to an end had me heated. I was racking my brain for an answer when I walked into the living room and told Seven to take the fat nigga to the basement. This house had nothing in it to tie this big nigga up with, so I was hoping he would go down there with no problem. He ended up not putting up that much of a fight, especially after Fish hit him in his mouth with the butt of his gun.

Once we got down there I stepped back and allow Seven and them to try and get the information I was looking for as I think. The way they were going it was going to take them all day. I wish I had Moose and Tots here with me. I get up and go upstairs, I was sure I saw a phone up there.

When I return they were still taking turns punching the nigga. I walk up and shoot the nigga in both shoulders. The yell was loud and long. I was in a rush but allowed the nigga to feel the pain.

"Seven hold him down and still." I say as I scroll through the in and out calls. With his forearm in the nigga's neck Seven got down and put all his weight on the nigga but it was evident that the nigga was done struggling. Throughout the beating he was saying he didn't know where Quan a.k.a. Flex was, I was believing him from the start I just allowed Seven to beat on him to soften him up.

"Which number is Flex?" I ask as I show him his call log. The nigga looked like he was about to go out so I smacked him and asked again. It took like ten seconds for him to focus, but he told me the first three digits and I found the number. After shooting him everybody else seemed to be more alert I noticed. The way Quan kept changing his numbers I was starting to feel like he was doing everything to avoid talking to me. I turned my back on the fat nigga and his pleas for medical help. I didn't wait to see if it was Quan on the phone or not.

"It's time to man up, Quan." I was talking calmly but fuming as I looked at Seven and them, looking back at me Seven was mouthing for me to ask about Cherry so I turned my back on him.

"Vegas! My baby I see you caught fat ass slipping." Quan sounded like he was happy and we were friends.

"Quan I'm done chasing you around. You acting like a real BITCH right now! Yeah you a real bitch nigga, titties and all, fuckin' fag!" I started laughing hoping to get him mad enough to jump out there.

"What Vegas!?! YOU WANT TO WILD WILD WEST THIS SHIT? Bitch that's what you want? Huh?" Quan yells through phone breathing hard. "Or how about we just call it even Vegas." I had to look at the phone, the change in his voice that sudden was crazy.

"Quan this ain't something we can settle over the phone. I need to look into your eyes and you mine so we can have a clear understanding." I made sure I sounded reasonable. This nigga was a mental mine, any false move and he could blow.

"You know Vegas... I can do that and really that's all I ever wanted to do." Quan took a deep breath and whispered to himself that he was tired.

"But Vegas, don't come on no bullshit! I'll hit yo hip about where to come." He transformed again before ending the call just like that. I'm not going to lie I was fucked up. This shit was weird.

Finally I was going to get this shit over with. My mind was already too focused on a more dangerous problem but I stopped it by turning back to Seven who was loaded with questions.

"Chill Seven! The nigga gonna call me and set up a meeting. It's probably gonna be some time ta'nite."

Seven had his face twisted up and he probably wanted more info on Cherry, but unlike Seven I knew that Quan wasn't just giving her back so asking about her was useless. I wasn't saying fuck her, but getting her back was a Seven problem not a Vegas problem.

"Seven I'mma hit yo hip when he hit mines. Then y'all meet me in front of The Holy Water." I do a one-eighty and head for the stairs.

"AY! Vegas wait! What's up with him?" Seven asks pointing to the fat nigga who was halfway dead...

"It's up to you. Leave him alive or kill him." I shrug and keep going up the stairs leaving the three niggas arguing.

CHAPTER 15

It was around nine and the clown Quan still hadn't called me. I was at my Ridgewood house throwing a glow in the dark ball around fucking with Tricks and Scar. Crazy she was chasing the ball and he was chasing her, I can see why they compare a nigga to a dog. I was chuckling at the scene when my phone started vibrating. The number was foreign to me, thinking it was finally Quan.

"Vegas, this Spokes!" Caught off guard but glad that Spokes finally tapped in, he sounded like he was out of breath.

"Nigga where you been and why you not calling from yo phone?" I'm unusually calm but I really was just happy to be hearing from Spokes. I wasn't worried worried, but I was beginning to wonder. Because I was thinking so much about Quan Spokes' whereabouts weren't a major concern until now.

"Man fucking with this bitch! All day I was on Lindsay fucking with this chick so I could keep an eye on Quan." Spokes had to take a breath. "The stupid bitch took my phone right before Quan came out so I left it with her and followed him." What the fuck!... I had to remind myself Spokes was only 13.

"So you still following him?"

"Yeah, I had to find somebody to let me make this call. Then I didn't know yo number so I had to hit that bitch up on Facebook but just listen Vegas, Quan's over here on the number streets. 24th he at an abandoned store it's big as fuck like two floors, I was in there." Of course he was! "I watched and heard him doing a drug deal with a dude in a grey Focus. I'm across the street from there now."

"Spokes, the nigga with the Focus, he still there too?"

"Yeah Vegas, the store is abandoned-looking but the inside not really fucked up. It looked like Quan was planning to turn it into an office or something." Damn I didn't have time to process all this.

"How many people with Quan?"

"Not including the two niggas in the Focus he got 5 with him, and he got Cherry. Vegas, she look bad too." Damn Spokes sounded sadder than Seven.

"Spokes, don't be a sucka. You did good even though I didn't ask you to. You could've got killed! Little nigga you gotta listen, fuck!" I had to stop before I cracked... damn I don't know where these emotions coming from.

"Alright this nigga looking like I'mma take off with his shit." Spokes ended the call, seconds later I was calling my dude.

Greybeard sounded like he was smoking on some of that strong shit they had over there on the number streets when he answered the phone.

"Vegas, what up doh! Heard you was putting in work over there."

"Greybeard you already know... I'm trying to hit yo hand tho, you feel me."

"Put me in position Boss Lady!" I had to chuckle, money get niggas attention quick.

"First tell me if you know a nigga named Quan or Flex?"

"Come on Vegas, you know I know muthafuckas, describe the nigga."

"Uhh, big-ass ugly tranny." Greybeard starts cracking up hard, yeah he was for sure blazing.

"Nah nah, Vegas, I don't know no trannies." He was lying about that but I believed he didn't know Quan.

"Alright fuck it. I want you to be ready to roll, you might want to be masked up since we in yo part of town." After running shit past Greybeard my next call was to Seven.

It was getting chilly so I put a black Nike sweat suit on over my shorts and jersey. Still popping pills like crazy only the drive to kill Quan had me up. I was determined to kill this nigga tonight!

I had Seven and his guys stay riding with him, I was in my Charger cruising down Livernois toward the number streets. I was hoping Quan hit me up before Spokes so I could get a sense of who I was dealing with. When I did get a call it was from another unknown number and it was Spokes telling me the Focus just left going back down toward the 30's. That's good, I hope Greybeard was in position. Shid he should be. I start speeding down Livernois. Looking in my rearview mirror I see Seven two cars behind in his truck. I didn't even ask Seven what he did with the fat nigga on Lindsay, I didn't even want to know.

Whenever I'm on a mission like this beforehand I make sure to line up some pussy for afterwards, if I make it. So I had Sara waiting up for me plus her brother was trying to link up. I had pussy and money lined up! Times like this the music game only had one nigga who could match this vibe consistently. I had to go to my Pooh Shiesty playlist. I was zoned out already seeing Quan's brains jumping outta his head looking like they running away from my hot hollows. Another unknown call; I was hoping it wasn't Spokes telling me Quan was on the move... It wasn't.

"Vegas, it's me, Flex." He was back to talking like a bitch. "It's late so let's do lunch tomorrow." This nigga sounding like an Atlanta Housewife.

"Come on Flex, nah let's do this ta'nite. That way tomorrow we can start fresh." I was trying to sound reasonable again, but I doubt it would last long!

"Really I just want to show you something ta'nite and you don't need to be here to see this." Slowing down I was making a left no more than a minute from Quan, he was talking but I was not really paying attention.

"Look Vegas! Vegas... Look!" Quan was yelling to get my attention he was definitely not Flex anymore. I look at my phone and Quan was showing me a table that looked similar to the one I had him chained to.

"Look familiar to you?" You could hear the amusement in his voice.

"Quan I thought we was squashing that ta'nite?" I was still trying to sound calm.

"Yeah, we is... If I recall right you had this bitch on the other end watching and listening." Quan gave Cherry some face time, she did look bad but not in the sense of beat up, she just looked torn down, high and dirty. I could only imagine how high she was. Cherry didn't drink or smoke since the last shit Quan did to her. I kept my mouth shut. It was evident that Quan thought he was in control.

"So now you gonna watch and listen as I fuck THIS BITCH IN THE ASS!" I could see he was high as a kite and ugly as a muthafucka! Arsenio Hall in Coming to America looking ass.

"Quan, I don't care about that bitch. I was in the room when Boots punished yo ass, I'm trying to be there and see you punish her... Now we can call Brittany, she's the only one who cares about Cherry, nigga." I was done trying to play his game. I was fuming as I hop out the Charger with my phone. I approach Spokes with my finger to my lips.

"Vegas, you right. But don't come here on some bullshit or I'mma fuck you over in here."

After Quan gave me the unnecessary info, since I was already across from him, I tell Spokes to take Mike and Fish in the way he got in and Seven and I were going to take the front door. I make sure they know don't start shooting for no reason.

From the outside you could see that the store was at least two floors. We make it just inside the doors and were met instantly

ALL GOOD A WEEK AGO

with .45's with extendos. I could tell this was probably once a grocery store, it was very spacious, so much so that you couldn't see the back wall from the door. The fact that it was dim played a part too, the smell of new paint was strong. Spokes was right, you could smell the newness coming off every object, desk, dividers, and the lamps that were sitting on the desks the few that were on gave the space its only light. Everything said Quan was trying to turn this into an office, probably had plans on a magazine or something. I didn't pay much attention to the guns pointing at me, wasn't the first time, plus Quan made it clear he wanted me to see this. Now Seven on the other hand looked a little shook, that was good... meant he was more likely to freeze up than jump the gun and that I could use; the jumping the gun I couldn't.

We continued deeper into the store and space started to widen to a space with no desks or dividers and there were ceiling lights instead of lamps. The scene that welcomed us was freaky in so many ways...

Cherry was bent over a steel table naked. Both her wrists were cuffed to rings coming from the table top and her ankles were cuffed to the legs of the table, she was whimpering quietly. Quan was behind her. He didn't have his usual lace front wig on. His hair was cut in a low fade. He had his shirt off and his perfect titties were sitting high in a push up bra. He was standing behind Cherry, he was actually trying to reenact the scene from the U-Haul unit to the point he was playing with his dick and talking to himself. I don't know if it was because they were waiting on me so Quan's goons weren't paying attention to Quan or because this was normal behavior on Quan's behalf so it wasn't that strange of a scene to them.

Like Spokes said Quan was surrounded by 5 niggas, regular looking niggas with guns. Two were on each side of him and two of the three guys who led us were now standing by the front of the table facing us and the fifth nigga was behind me. He was the one I was worried about.

Quan finally looked up from the prep talk to his dick and he went from looking like sick nigga to a sick bitch.

"Vegas! So you did bring company." Quan, or was it Flex, who looked at Seven like he was seeing something he liked.

"You didn't say I couldn't bring somebody, plus I thought it would make you happy if he saw this too." Hearing my voice Cherry looked up. Her eyes got big when they finally focused and she saw Seven.

"Rio!" Cherry called Seven's name in a hoarse plea. I had to be quick when Seven took a long lunge toward the table, causing pain to shoot through my body by grabbing and containing his big ass. When he looked at me, even if I wasn't holding him, you could see him visibly shaking and tears were running down his face.

"Seven you got to calm down or you're going to get yourself killed along with Cherry." Making sure I leave myself out of it as I tell Seven this firmly but in a whisper.

"Oohh! So this must be her meat. Vegas, you don't know how much you fucked me up… LOOK AT ME!" I had to take a step back, the easy transformation in voice and demeanor was spooky. He went from Flex to Quan; he went from pointing his gun down to pointing it at me, and I never took my eyes from his as I raise my hands.

"Man, you might want to move from behind me before he shoot and miss." I tell the nigga behind me hoping I sounded scared and worried, neither of which I felt.

"Yeah, get from behind her. That's Vegas, she ain't doing no running. And nobody better not even aim at her! So nigga this yo bitch huh? Well you gonna stand there and watch as I fuck her in the ass." Quan set his gun on Cherry's back now that we were closer I could hear her and she was praying. Even for a cold blooded muthafucka like me seeing Cherry in that position was pulling at my soul. Quan just bought himself a full clip!

CHAPTER 16

As his five shooters were watching us I was watching Quan spread Cherry's ass cheeks while the whole time complimenting her on her pretty chocolate ass.

"My mans, I wish you could see this. You know I'm going to do you better than how Vegas did me. Here Cherry, spit in my hand." Quan said as he bent forward putting his hand in front of Cherry's mouth. She ignored it...

Upstairs just then Mike and Fish showed themselves. Not fully but we made eye contact. I was happy not to see Spokes, one less muthafucka to worry about.

"Fuck it then!" Quan says before he takes his time entering Cherry's back door. The scream Cherry let out wasn't as deafening as Quan's was, or maybe I just didn't enjoy hearing her as much so it didn't seem as loud. You could see it on Quan's face going in dry was painful for him too.

Cherry was loudly protesting and Seven was slowly easing his way forward. I had to pull him back a few times. Five niggas with guns pointing at him, it's not like he was going to sneak up on them, the fuck he thinking!

Quan was now roughly pounding Cherry, the scene got wilder as Quan kept switching from growling in a man's voice to moaning in a female voice.

"VEGAS!" Quan screamed my name and point his gun at me.

"AHHH!" Quan yells, now pointing the gun at himself. Quan repeated this three times. As he was doing this Mike and Fish worked their way quickly down the stairs, Quan's yelling and Cherry's pleas were covering whatever sound they did make.

"Vegas, you want me to buss in this bitch?" Quan asks repeating the same question Boots asked when he was deep in his ass. I didn't know what Quan was really asking cause just then he was pressing his gun to Cherry's head. It seemed Seven didn't know either because he chose that time to pull out a six-shooter. A FUCKIN' SIX-SHOOTER! I knew shit was gonna end bad for him then, so I did the only smart thing I could. It seemed like things were moving in slow-motion. When Seven raised his gun at Quan, his goons were aiming at Seven. Mike and Fish were coming at full speed now. So the smart thing for me was to pull out my gun and simultaneously we were all shooting... Seven at Quan, Mike and Fish at Quan's goons, Quan's goons were shooting at Seven, and I was shooting and launching for the nigga closest to me, the one who was minutes ago behind me. I was hoping he'll fall dead from my head shot and I could use his body for some type of cover. I didn't know who Quan was aiming at or if he was aiming at all. Last time I saw him he was smiling while he rammed Cherry from behind...

***

"Vegas, get up. You safe." Yes, just the voice I was hoping not to hear once the shooting stopped and my ears stopped ringing...

A fucking six-shooter, fuckin' Dirty Harry ass nigga, shi-it at least he had a fo-fo!

I was laying under the dead nigga I shot. I was pissed and at a major disadvantage. Hearing Quan's voice I toss the dead weight off me and slowly get up. I was in pain, but not that bad. I took stock of the chaos around me. In less than 20 seconds everybody was down. Seven was only a foot, maybe two, from where he was standing before he went for Quan. A fuckin' six-shooter, I couldn't wait to tell this story. It looked like Seven killed one of the niggas at the front of the table. Mike and Fish took out the two niggas next to Quan, it took most of their bullets before Quan and the only nigga left killed them. Quan got grazed and the other nigga looked like he got hit in the chest, but Quan had all his dudes vested up. I was covered in blood. Somebody was shooting at me and my human shield caught everything, but I still got up limping moving slowly. To my surprise Cherry was still alive too.

"Vegas my baby, you alright?" There he go again sounding like Nene Leeks.

"Yeah Flex, I'm cool but one of yo fuck boys was shooting at me!" Flex was easier to manipulate than Quan, if that made sense. No longer paying me any attention Quan was back playing with his dick. I still had one of my guns in my holster but Quan's goon was activated, he wasn't missing nothing.

"Now let's finish this." Quan placed his gun back on Cherry's back and enter her. Cherry didn't scream this time, in a trance-like state she kept repeating Seven's name and how sorry she was.

"Yeah bitch, call me his name! Mario, sorry Mario." Flex was back, he wasn't mocking Cherry, he was moaning and talking as if he was Cherry. His eyes were wide open and he looked like he was catching his second buzz from whatever he was sniffing earlier. He was back to pointing his gun from me to Cherry and then to himself like he was playing eenie-meenie-minie-moe.

"Vegas, you see what you did to me! Look at me Vegas... My titties, you like them?" It was crazy he was going from sounding like a man in Quan's voice to sounding like Flex in a woman's voice. He was gone and the way he was sounding and moving he was on the verge of nutting.

"You want me to buss in this bitch, huh? Buss in this bitch, buss in this bitch! Come on, come on! Buss in this bitch, come on, come on!" Quan was reciting this as he sped up his pumps, Cherry was out of her mind, her eyes were open but they weren't in focus.

"Buss in her... Buss in... This BITCH!"
BLAAA!
The shot was so sudden it froze me and Quan's goon. Cherry's brains decorated the steel table...
Flex was back and he was moaning with his gun pointed my way as he recovered from what looked like a powerful nut.
"Vegas, who was shooting at you huh? After this we gonna be best friends. I'm sorry for putting that ticket on your head." Flex stepped back his now soft dick falling out of Cherry's ass, his gun still pointed at me. I made sure not to look down.
"I remember telling everybody, 'DON'T SHOOT AT VEGAS!' Now who was it?" Flex yelled as he looked around as if he was now realizing everybody was dead.
"Oh, I guess it's just you, Fein, and me... Fein? You shoot at Vegas, huh?" Fein looked towards Flex. You could see the fear in his eyes, I guess he was as uncertain as me but I was ready like I said, I still had a gun on me. I had to be ready and quick, cowboy style.
"Fein, you shoot at Vegas!" This time it wasn't a question. Flex still had his gun on me and his eyes were wild. I started to ease my hand up. Me and Fein were both looking at Flex or Quan, I don't know who I was dealing with right now, but his anger was building...
When I spoke I kind of whispered but I made sure I was loud enough for Quan/Flex to hear me. "Fein, I seen you shoot at me."
After this I was as ready as I ever have been for anything to happen. When Quan/Flex swung his gun toward Fein and shot him, he may have been too slow to swing his gun around, but I wasn't, and I quickly pull my gun from my holster and let off two shots hitting Quan in the shoulder as he was swinging back toward me cause his gun to go flying past me.
Flex stumbled and fell over one of his shooters. I didn't run, but I moved quickly and made it over there just in time to kick the gun from his reach before shooting him twice in his stomach. The vest stopped it from penetrating but from experience I knew

ALL GOOD A WEEK AGO

the pain he was in. I pulled Quan by his bullet riddled arm and dragged him to the open space nowhere near a gun. I was loving the sound of his screaming and I was talking as I searched for my other gun.

"You fucked up Quan, you went down South and you forgot who I was... Thought you could play the cat and mouse game with my life." I pick up my gun and pop the clip as I walk toward Quan. He was pleading, but I ignored him.

"I made myself a couple promises. First, thanks for making me feel more at home. I needed this." I say to Quan as I stand over him refilling one of my clips. Nines are known to jam so I wasn't gonna risk it and put one in the chamber. "Before ta'nite I promised you 5 to the head but you earned yourself a whole clip for that shit you did to Cherry, so good for you." I say in a cheerful voice as I aim my pistol at Quan and unload the whole clip Sicario style at his crying face...

I was cruising down West Warren coming from Sara's brother's crib. After the Quan shit I went over there as planned. Sara's brother Sam was trying to move about 200 guns. He had this big-ass .50 cal revolver I was for sure taking off his hands. It was four in the morning, I read somewhere that this was the coldest and quietest time in the day. I don't know how true it was but it was proving to be true now. I was too wired to sleep, my day started with some pussy so I was already on the up-trend. I was just turning down Grand River heading for my loft, driving in the middle of the lane so it was easy for the two Sprinter vans to box me in, but shid I was in a Charger SRT Super Stock, ain't no way! I push the gas as I look over to the van on my left. I was passing them when the doors opened up and just barely I see Gage bound and gagged! My mind was moving just as fast as my car, nothing was forming... "Fuck!"

I slow down but don't stop. I was now doing 25mph...

I stopped, making sure I was still many blocks from downtown. I didn't turn off the car. It wasn't long before the van pulled up and two figures in black hop out with AR15 pistols aimed at me. I was in a bullet proof car but I doubt if I could take too many of them.

"Apaga el cario! Apaga el cario!" One of the gunman yells for me to turn my car off. Damn Vee… I take a deep breath wishing I could shoot through the door. I turn the car off.

After what felt like forever with two AR15's aimed at me a black Bentley Coupe pulls up on the other side of the van. I couldn't see who was in it. Both van doors open and no surprise, Gage is pulled from one of them, the big surprise for me was that Rev and Joyce were pulled out of the other one. Neither looked hurt or anything, but Rev looked pissed and Joyce looked scared. There was no coming back from this if they were smart they'll kill us all right here and now. A woman comes from the other side of the car. She was dressed in an all-black dress, tight and showing off all her curves. I knew that body anywhere. In this quiet moment her heels made it sound like she was walking to a beat, but it wasn't to the beat of my heart pounding because if it was she'd be running, that's how fast my shit was beating! It's been years since I saw Lorimar, today she had on a black veil covering her face as if in mourning. No matter, I knew it was her. She stopped in front of my Charger and my light made the scene look like a showdown in a movie.

The gunmen pushed Gage and Joyce towards Lorimar, they both went along with no problem as if they knew what I knew. Lorimar raised the veil from her face and there she was, still as beautiful as ever, but I was too full of anger to be drunk by her beauty…

"How you doing Vegas?" Her accent was heavier since the last time I spoke to her.

"A debt is owed and it's time for you to pay it." Her voice was calm and full of emotions, Lorimar held out her hand and one of her gunmen placed a baby 45 in it.

"A fake mother or a fake brother don't add up to my Jose… but I did love you once… Choose!"

WHAT!?! I can't believe this, I lay my head on the steering wheel. I had no intentions of choosing. Both Gage and Joyce were shaking and crying. Neither said anything and that was a small blessing. If I chose or didn't it didn't make a difference because there was no right answer. So I did the only thing I could, I put on an 'I don't care' expression and shrugged. Lorimar put the gun to Joyce's head and I heard Rev let out a low groan/growl.

I put my head back down. I didn't want to see knowing this was all my fault.

"BLAAKA!"

My head shot up as Gage was dropping to the ground. "Nooooo!" My yell was cut off by a cry in my throat as tears flowed down my face. The feeling was indescribable. Never in my 27 years have I ever felt it, so how could I describe or name it?

Instead of down I held my head up and allowed my feelings to show. If Lorimar knew me then she knew her death could never be that fast.

"I'll take them home and let you take care of Gage, Vegas. But I'll be in touch." Bitch had the nerve to be crying... I didn't acknowledge her in any way. I kept my head straight and waited until they were gone. I got out of my Charger and opened the back door before going to pick up Gage. Damn, he might've been light alive, but in death he was heavy as hell. I got him to my back seat and instead of going to my loft I turned the car around...

It's been three days since Gage was murdered in front of me. After getting Gage's body in my back seat I called my guy who owns a funeral home on Dexter and went straight there. I was thinking more clearly that day than I thought I would've after seeing Gage killed, I can't explain it. At the funeral home I had to wait for my guy but it didn't take long.

Once in the funeral home my guy knew I wasn't there to make normal arrangements. Nothing about this was normal, but with me being the only family Gage had I just told him I wanted him cremated and to call me once he finished so I can pick up the ashes and then I left...

I haven't left my loft since picking up his ashes, with no one but Sara knowing about my loft she stopped by but at once she knew not to come back, to just give me some time. Now I was only being bothered with phone calls, and I answered them all. I wasn't hiding, I was just regrouping. Everyone seemed to take offense to how I handled the Gage situation before and after he was killed. The fact that I didn't at least have a small gathering in his memory felt wrong to them. But FUCK'EM! That's how I was feeling. Tots wanted to come home but I deaded that. I told her I was fine, and I was, yeah I cried the first two days but like Rev says life goes on.

All the things I bought for my loft were coming in and that's been keeping me busy these past three days. Rev's been calling and giving me updates on the remodeling of the Holy Water, he hasn't said a word about Lorimar kidnapping him and Joyce, but that's a story I'm waiting to hear. It was sunny today and I was planning to step out. Gage was dead and that was that. Quan was dead, so that case was closed too. This past week had its ups and downs, but I was fully back now, and Lorimar said she'll be in touch, and I couldn't wait!

TO BE CONTINUED…

COMING SOON...

IN MY LIFETIME... VOL 2 FRENEMIES

PREVIEW: CHAPTER 1

Flashback: The Meeting

"JIMMY STOP RUNNING!" Damn I hate these dope Fein's one thing for sure I didn't quit being a undercover to chase Fein's. Jimmy was moving like 40mph it seem, while screaming "ALIENS" at the top of his lungs. The only good thing so far is that he running in a straight line...

He was a nice distance in front of me, mid-October one in the afternoon so as expected it was wet, damp and a ghost town. Ahead of me Jimmy slides across an abandon car, when I got to it I just ran around it while Jimmy was making a sharp turn. "FUCK!" I could see this muthafucka wasn't slowing down forcing me to get in my track and field mode. Jimmy was still yelling but I no longer could decipher a word.

Damn I didn't know trailers had gates but the one Jimmy was running towards did. I was right behind him now like 30 feet apart. The yard was junky, muddy and full of bike parts Jimmy seem unfazed by any of it while I was jumping and dodging shit left and right. Leaving the junky yard through the back we were crossing what seem to be the Trailer Park street before I was back to chasing him between trailers.

Just as we were nearing the back of one trailer home out of nowhere came some steaming water catching Jimmy in the face. Letting out a unhuman sound he begun spinning and throwing punches...

"GET OFF ME! AHHH!"

This white boy high as fuck I was thinking while diving at him hitting him with a Goldberg spear tackling him to the muddy ground...

On the ground I wrestled with Jimmy for a while it was clear he was stronger than me and high, working in his favor also was the unbearable stench coming from him! The smell of old pork and fishy dish water...

Finally I got the upper hand putting my forearm in Jimmy's throat before punching in him in his scab peeling face...

"Jimmy, JIMMY! Chill the fuck out!" I say through clenched teeth as I put more pressure on his throat hoping he comes to his senses. Jimmy's wide eyes showed just a little fear.

"Who are you... Ahh! Who are you!" Jimmy started struggling so I punched him again and again, with the yard being muddy it was hard for me to keep the upper hand and he finally got on top of me and hit me with two powerful shots to the jaw...

I wasn't given the chance to take a breath or two when Jimmy stood up because it only took a second for him to pull out a big-ass kitchen knife... "OH SHIT!" Man where the fuck he hide that at? Usually I'll have a pistol on me but when I turned in my budge they suspended my license to carry and right now I was still under investigation by Internal Affairs.

I was alert enough to hear a motorcycle roaring through the Trailer Park, happy knowing it was Foureyes. After quitting the force I was offered a chance to join a Biker Gang called the Landsharks, a multi-culture biker gang who dealt in drugs, guns and property. Foureyes is my uncle that brought me in... Well right now I'm just a Goldfish A.K.A. a Prospect.

So that's why I'm in this Trailer Park weaponless squaring up with a spaced-out junkie with a kitchen knife named Jimmy trying to collect money from the so-called dealer. Not for the first time just the first time I caught him after taking a blast. My only hope was to stay out his way until Foureyes showed up. But that muthafucka better hurry up!

"You see I knows you-s alien... but I ain't going back on that U.F.O." Jimmy's voice was shaky and his eyes were wild he was taking a few steps forward while I was stepping back trying to figure out how to convince him I'm not an alien. I don't know how skilled he is with a knife but he looked real comfortable with it in his hand.

"Jimmy just calm down it's me Vegas... I'm not an alien." I wasn't scared but I was less comfortable without my gun. Jimmy was high and instead of calming down he lunged at me and slashed. Damn that was close but I was quick enough to side step and catch him with a jab, it felt good too! Stumbling a little bit before getting his footing and coming at me again too high to learn from his mistake we repeated... He lunges... I pivot... I jab... By the time Foureyes showed up we was on our fourth sequence I could've been did something different. I could've waited until he slash, kicked him in the knee and step into a powerful left hook, which I did on the fifth series. Jimmy went down with a loud "FUCK!"

"CLICCLACK!"... Hearing a shotgun being cocked froze me.

"Black bitch, naw what you think you doing in my yard beating on Jimmy!" Shit I hope this brotherfucker don't shoot me I think as I peek a look at Foureyes who look less concern than me. Either because he knew something I didn't or because the brotherfucker wasn't aiming whatever she was holding at him.

"Nigger what you-s deaf!"

"No miss I hear ya." I calmly says as I slowly turn around with my hands up smiling. The fat white bitch was holding an old-ass 12" gage looking very comfortable with it in her hands standing in slippers and a dirty house robe.

"Now listen-..."

"Vegas!" Hearing the urgency in Foureyes's voice caused me to turn around on guard so I was able to dodge the wild left hand punch but wasn't lucky enough to escape the knife slash to my abdomen which caused a instant burn. The slash took most of the power outta my hook that connected with Jimmy's face...

CHAPTER 2

Foureyes still brings that up whenever I see him at a Club meeting it's an easy way for him to point out how he saved my life which he really did when he blew off the fat bitch face. That was last year, now I'm in Ashely Hair Salon looking at my fresh fauxhawk in the big mirror. She was on her shit ta'day my line up was crispy and my curly black honey streak hawk had a nice bounce to it she earned that tip and if she stop faking it'll be my pleasure to replace that money with my tongue. That thought got me chuckling... I had to admit I'm a fine muthafucka and everything looked good in my Gucci sports bra and Gucci joggers, my thickness was very noticeable at 5'10" and 150lbs. Also what was noticeable was the long-ass scar left by those 12 staples from that slash from Jimmy on the side of my 6-pack. Reason for my reminiscing of that day.

"Ashely you was fuckin with me ta'day!" I say this as I turn from the mirror, as expected before noon on a Tuesday the shop was light weight empty. Muthafuckas was at work! Something I was out of as I still wait for my P.I. licenses, shi-it with my connections in the street and the Detroit Police Force being a P.I. was the next best thing I could do. Especially how I was planning to do it. I'm about to take the city over like never before.

"Huh Vegas?" Ashely put her hands on her hips and snap her neck like them bitches do fake mad. This bitch knew she was fucking me up with those light brown eyes.

"What I fucked you up last time?" I couldn't do nothing but smile, shake my head and bite my lip.

"Yeah! Now sit back down and let me line your back up."

"You talkin to me like you my bitch."

"Yeah you wish."

"Wont you play genie and grant it then... I promise to rub you right." I say putting on my Fresh Prince...

(Chuckling)... "Unum! Vegas you wouldn't kno what to do I let yo young ass taste this... shit addictive trust." Ashely says as she lightly rub my ear before pushing my head down slightly to line me up. She was in her mid-30's, that's her favorite thing teasing me then bringing up my age I'm 24. But I'll fuck her mind up before she fuck mines up.

"So what was you thinking that had you smiling like that over there in the mirror?" I was about to answer her when this bad-ass Spanish bitch came in. She was about 5'6", 5'7" with heels on, Versace sunglasses and a Versace scarf covering her hair look like more for style than need. Her body wasn't super thick but it was curvy and well portion the type of body you just knew fit perfectly in your hands no matter where you hold her at.

Her white Versace sundress looked like it was made tailored for her and she was carrying a Versace bag. You couldn't call it nothing but a bag, a purse wouldn't described it right. She looked pissed when she took her glasses off and looked around like I said the salon was damn near empty. There were only two other Stylists in and they had clients but none of the nail techs were here. The Spanish chick looked as if she expected to walk into a chair she mumbled something in Spanish but she was still by the door well out of my hearing range. With her glasses off she was a dead look-a-like for Roselyn Sanchez I'll still take J-Lo when it come to old bad-ass Spanish chicks but ole girl was up there for me.

Before she said a word I knew she was a boss bitch and I could do nothing but follow her with my eyes as she walked toward my chair. Our eyes met for a brief second I'm not shy or aggressive when it comes to female and I never have to say much for one to know how I felt so when she took me in in that second no doubt she knew I was liking what I was looking at.

"She must be important for you to book her in my slot Ashely." Her tone didn't match the irritation in her face and DAMN this bitch smelled good! After watching her since she walked in I turned forward taking the time to try to come up with something to say whenever the moment presented itself.

"Yeah… I was just touching her up I'll be done in a second." Damn Ashely was so business-like, this woman must really be the important one.

"I got stuff to do in the back anyways." That accent was killing me and I think she was putting it on thick for me, facts she put a little extra in her walk when she cross my visual. Her perfect ass cheeks was swallowing up her thong. Damn! It's something about white, dress, pants it didn't matter that color do something crazy for a female shape.

Ashely had a dial pad with fingerprint recognition for entry to the office. I always wondered about that and seeing this Spanish chick there now repiqued my curiosity, bag and all. When her fingerprint didn't catch she looked at me I was looking straight but she was hip to me watching I believe. Hearing the front door opening I look toward it and two masked-up niggas was coming in pointing big-ass sticks, fuck words they came straight in and the first person aimed my way and fired. "BLAH!"

I was surprise to still be alive feeling blood splattered on my neck and shoulder as Ashely was dome checked. I wasn't shocked but I was smart so I didn't say nothing and kept my head down. Though it was clear these niggas was on a mission because as the other customers and workers screamed and went to the floor the shooter ignore them and me.

"Put the bag down and move to the corner, hurry the fuck up!" Ole girl didn't look spooked at all and kept her eyes on the shooter with a smirk on her sexy-ass face as she dropped the Versace bag and slowly backed into a corner as instructed. The other masked figure ran and grabbed the bag without another word they both left the shop quickly, followed seconds by the screaming customers and workers…

It was dead silence no pun intended it felt like minutes before either of us spoke. I was still in my chair she was just now leaving her corner.

"You going to call the cops?" I had to respect her calmness.

"Shit, evidently this yo establishment." I matched her tone and it caused us both to smile before she dial the cops on her cell, which was the first time I notice it in her hand...

"Vegas Wolfchild!" I put my head down in pure irritation hearing Detective Rooney's voice. How quickly the cops got here I was sure one of the crying muthafuckas called before the Spanish chick did. We both been questioned by the beat cops and Rooney was just finishing up with the Spanish chick I wasn't really in the mood for another series of questions. Ashely's blood only got on my shoulder and neck and even though the paramedic cleaned me up good I still felt disgusting. Now hearing Rooney addressing me only added to my irritation but I put a smile on my face still when I turned around.

"I answered questions already. I'm leaving." Rooney was already smiling before I finish, shaking his head as I pass him with plans on learning the Spanish chick's name now that he was done with her she was standing in front of the office.

"I figure since we shared this tragedy together it's only right that I learn your name." I say once I'm close enough to touch her but I don't of course.

"My name?" That accent was so sexy and the smile she was giving me had my nipples getting hard.

"Yeah I need to know your name, I can't keep referring to you in my head as the sexy Spanish chick." Her smile widened.

"Well Vegas Wolfchild... I'm Lorimar." She said my name so sexy I wasn't irked by it but turned on so when she reached out a hand and instead of shaking it I caressed it and gave her a smile with thoughts of her pretty manicured fingers on my throbbing clit. The contact was shortened by some pretty boy Spanish type nigga coming in calling Lorimar mother. I turned and left.

About the Author

My name is Clay Church. I'm 36 years old and I've been in federal custody for 16 years. I was born and raised in Detroit, Michigan. I recently found my love for writing and years ago I started with All Good a Week Ago and this great character Vegas Wolfchild. This is just a small portion of Vegas, not enough to fill you up but to make you hunger for more, which is coming. I hope you enjoy this book. Thanks.